INSUBORDINATE BASTARD
A WWII Soldier's Story

Janet Flickinger-Bonarski

First Edition

45th Parallel Publishing Co. Gaylord, Michigan

Insubordinate Bastard
A WWII soldier's story

Published by:
45th Parallel Publishing Co.
PMB 182
1429 West Main
Gaylord, MI 49735

Copyright 2002 by Janet Flickinger-Bonarski
Cover by Angela Underwood – www.booksindesign.com

ISBN 0-9716793-0-4
First Printing, 2002

Publisher's Cataloging-in-Publication
(Provided by Quality Books, Inc.)

Flickinger-Bonarski, Janet.
    Insubordinate bastard : a WWII soldier's story /
Janet Flickinger-Bonarski. -- 1st ed.
    p. cm.
    ISBN 0-9716793-0-4

    1. Willet, Gerald--Fiction. 2. World War, 1939-1945
--Oceania--Fiction. 3. Americans--Oceania--Fiction.
4. Soldiers--Fiction. 5. Oceania--Fiction.
6. Biographical fiction. 7. War stories. I. Title.

PS3606.L53I57 2002   813'.6
                    QBI02-200023

For my Step-father, Gerald, and my husband, Richard, both of whom have always been the wind beneath my wings.

PREFACE

Insubordinate Bastard is a fictionalized biography of my stepfather, Gerald Willet, during World War II. The various incidents in the book are based on the "war stories" I heard told and re-told at family gatherings during the 1950's when I was growing up.

Gerald's brother, Frank, urged me to put the stories together. "It brings out some of the funny situations we encountered while living in fox holes and parts of the story you don't generally hear." Since Frank had also served in the Pacific Theater during World War II, he was able to help me with details, and add parts of the stories I had not heard.   The characters in the story are based on people Gerald talked about, but all the characters, with the exception of General William Chase, whom he greatly admired, and the First Sergeant, whose name I have changed, are composite creations of my own.

The stories show Gerald as I knew him, a kind man who truly cared about others, but who was capable of, and insisted upon, thinking for himself.

Janet Bonarski

Ft. Riley, Kansas
December 1941 to June 1942

Corporal George Lewis sat at the table, his lip pulled tightly over his lower teeth. His tongue played with the rolled surface as he read. Patsy Goodwin, the girl he'd left behind on December 9, 1941, would have known it was a sign of impatience. The headlines all week had detailed the Japanese navy moving across the South Pacific. Last Monday it was YANKS CHASE ENEMY SHIPS. Friday it had been JAP AIRCRAFT CARRIER DAMAGED IN RAID ON MIDWAY. Now today, Monday, 8 June 1942, it was FRUSTRATED JAPS ESCAPE U.S. FLEET.

"Roger?" he addressed his companion across the table.

"What?" Roger answered without interrupting his review of the Blondie comic strip.

"Doesn't it bother you that we're stuck here at Ft. Riley drilling troops while all this action is going on?"

"What action?" Roger asked, still reading comic strips.

"Listen to this. 'Pacific pursuit wanes with damage to foe reported heavy.' We're starting to win, Rog, and it'll all be over before I ever get to take part in it."

"Good, then I can go home and marry Shirley." He lowered the newspaper and looked keenly at George. He knew by the look in those flashing black eyes that George was planning something. George knocked the long ash from his cigarette and made a face at the bitter taste of the cold coffee.

"I didn't enlist in this army to drill troops," George said. "I enlisted to fight. If they won't let me fight, I'm going to go home."

Roger laughed out loud, his large hand slapping the tabletop. "Go home? What regulation you going to find that'll let you just go home?"

He was referring to the way George read and used obscure army regulations to thwart the establishment. Being able to cite regulations word for word was one way George used his photographic memory. The fact that he read regulations at all was unusual for an enlisted man and stemmed both from his love of reading and his desire to know the rules he was expected to follow.

"I'm not supposed to be here," George replied. "I'm so color blind I don't know what color this table is, or if the traffic lights out there are red or green, except by their positions. I only got in because they were careless on the day after Pearl. I tried to enlist in the Navy a year before, but they wouldn't take me and told me none of the other services would either. All I have to do is arrange to have an eye test and let them find out I'm color-blind."

Roger groaned and picked up his paper again. "Why do you want to go fight, maybe get yourself killed?"

George tapped the newspaper article with his left forefinger. "When those Jap bastards dropped their bombs on Pearl Harbor it felt to me as if they'd dropped them in Lake Michigan. I'm willing to die, if that's what it takes, to keep this land of ours free."

"Well I'm not," retorted the other man. "We're safe here and we're doing our part. I don't understand this urge to suicide you have."

"It's honor, not suicide. A family tradition. When my mother died and Dad decided to keep the family together, we all pitched in and did our part. My brothers have all been shipped overseas already. Even my sister, Ellen, an officer in the WACS, is in England. I refuse be the only one who had a cushy job state side."

Roger and George had passes to go into Junction City on the following Saturday. They were part of the mollification package Sgt. Blake had offered along with the promotion to corporal on his third denial of George's request for a transfer. They both wore their best blitzed up uniforms. It was Roger's idea to have their pictures taken.

"Shirley deserves a picture of such a good looking Corporal" he said when they spotted a portrait studio with a sign in the window promising one week processing. "How 'bout you? You don't want Patsy to forget you, do ya?"

George agreed, even though he didn't think he'd be around next week to pick it up. He let himself be led into the portrait studio.

"Let's do it now if we're going to, before my five o'clock shadow is visible," he said.

George had black hair, flashing black eyes, and a black beard that began to shadow his face well before five each afternoon. They paid the photographer for three single poses and two of both of them together. George was shorter than average, barely five foot seven, while Roger was sandy haired and five foot eleven. The photographer posed them side by side for one shot and Roger standing slightly behind George for the other. They'd met the first day in basic training and been friends immediately. Both had been in Roosevelt's depression work program for young men, the Civilian Conservation Corp. George had served in Northern Michigan, and Roger in Oregon, and at twenty-eight, they were older than most of the other men.

After the pictures they stopped at the Rexall Drug store so George could pick up some reading material. He found two Zane Grey novels he hadn't read. He was looking forward to a long train ride and wanted something to read on the way. Roger bought a "Field and Stream" magazine.

"Let's grab some grub before we start celebrating," Roger said.

They went into Molly's Diner where they each had a plate of beef stew. While they were eating, Abe Johnson and Dave Wilson, both from their company, came in.

"Hey," Roger hailed them. Abe slid into the booth next to Roger. Dave, a tall lanky boy, stood at the end of the table and nervously turned his hat in his hands.

George moved over and patted the seat beside him. "Sit," he said, and like an obedient dog, Dave sat, but perched on the edge of the seat with legs in the aisle and his back to George.

"You fellas up to anything?" Abe asked.

"Not yet," Roger said. "You got anything in mind?"

"Like to find some girls," Dave said. He said it with his head down and turned away from the table. George noticed the back of his neck redden when he said it.

"Me and Roger have girls back home," George said. "We had more in mind to go to a movie." It would be better for his plan to get rid of these two, he thought. Roger too. Maybe these guys' showing up was a good thing.

"There's a dance at the Armory," Abe said. "Let's go there and see what's happening." They talked over other options and finally decided on the dance.

They had walked half a block when George stopped suddenly, "I need to go back to the Rexall. It's my sister's birthday next week and I should have gotten her a card. I'll catch up with you."

At the corner, George turned and watched until the trio crossed the street. Then he started looking for a suitable juke-joint. He wandered around checking out the bars until he found a small one called the Bomber, sandwiched between two loud noisy joints. It was full of GI's and local girls. A Benny Goodman song played on the jukebox. After checking to make sure there was nobody he knew, he sat down at an empty table just inside the door.

He gathered up all the empty long neck bottles he could and filled the table with them. He let the waitress bring him a beer, lit a Lucky, and settled in to wait.

He stopped the waitress when she tried to clear the table for him. "When my buddies show up, I want them to think I've been here a long, long time," he told her. She winked at him and added a few more from her tray.

The jukebox switched to Larry Clinton and his orchestra playing Deep Purple. Here and there, couples got up to dance to the slow music. George sat back to watch them and thought of Patsy, his black-haired fiancée. This was their song. George wasn't any good at the fast dances, but he and Patsy danced every slow one. Patsy had wanted to get married before he left, but George thought it would be better to wait until the war was over. Besides, she was just out of high school, almost nine years younger than he , and she needed some time to make sure she wanted him.

He'd been nursing one beer for almost an hour when two MP's appeared on their rounds. As soon as they stuck their heads in the door, George stood up, kicked his chair over, and began to stagger. He knocked over the table filled with empty bottles. The crash brought an instant halt to the low undertone of voices in the bar.

He felt the MP's beside him and heard one of them say, "I think you've had too much to drink, Corporal. Let me..."

George shook the MP's hands off and slapped him across the face with his open palm. His left-handedness had caught them off guard. Quick as a flash, the other MP pinned George's arms behind him. He quit struggling and let them take him outside. The night was warm, and the nearly full moon was visible above the top of the filling station across the street.

By morning the guard house was full of men in various stages of recovery after a night of drinking. At ten o'clock, the MP's escorted George to the provost marshal's office in the base headquarters building.

It would be a summary court, where one commissioned officer acted as judge, jury, and prosecutor. Besides George and the MP's there was only a court recorder. They seated George at a table in front of the railing dividing the accused from the spectators. Soon a major entered. George stood at attention. The officer sat down behind a heavy oak table on a slightly raised platform in the front of the room. There was an oak bookcase lined with large books behind him, an American flag to one side, and a round metal wastebasket to the left of the table. He nodded for George to sit.

Major Holt looked very military with straight posture and not a hair out of place. He fixed George with a look of assumed superiority George thought all officers had. Holt cleared his throat and spoke in a voice too loud for the room.

"State your name, rank, serial number, and company, soldier."

"Corporal George Lewis, 16027305, Delta Company of the 402nd recruit instructor battalion, Ft. Riley, Kansas, SIR."

The charges were read: "Cpl. Lewis, you are charged with being drunk and disorderly in a public place and striking a military policeman. How do you plead?"

"Guilty, Sir."

"Very well, Corporal, you may sit down. Do you request to be represented by an advocate?"

Last thing in the world he wanted, some hot shot defense advocate messing things up. "No Sir," he answered.

"Well then," the major said, "we will proceed according to regulations."

Exactly what he wanted to hear.

The major flipped through George's file, reading the record of his six months of military life. When he'd finished reading, he removed his glasses and leaned forward. "These papers indicate that you have been a recruit instructor for four months and were just awarded your promotion two weeks ago. How do you explain yourself?" He replaced the glasses and sat back to listen.

"Just celebrating a little too hard, Sir." George said.

"You have violated the military code of conduct for a non-commissioned officer of the army. This is a non-criminal violation so there will be no guardhouse time. However, regulations leave me no choice but to reduce you to the grade of private."

George almost breathed a sigh of relief. His worse fear was that he would be reduced just one grade to private first class

The major peered over the top of his glasses, perhaps looking for some sign of remorse. George was struggling to keep from gloating.

"That will be all, Private, you are dismissed."

But ex-Corporal George W. Lewis wasn't finished.

"Sir", he said, "Excuse me, but army regulation AR-700-1722 states that when a non-commissioned officer is reduced to the grade of private for a non-criminal violation, he has the right to request transfer to an assignment of his choice within forty-eight hours."

Holt had been half way out of his chair, but he sat down again with a heavy thud. A surprised "What?" escaped from his mouth before he reassumed his military demeanor. He sat very rigid and stared at George for a minute, then got up and began to search the bookshelves for the book that contained the regulation George had cited. George thought he'd never forget the expression of surprise and disbelief on the major's face as he read. George had quoted it word for word.

"How did you know about this regulation, private?" he asked.

"I came across it when I was reading the regulations, Sir,"

"Do you 'read regulations' often?" His tone was both sarcastic and incredulous.

"I've read many of them, Sir. I find them interesting and informative."

Major Holt shook his head. "I'm sure you do," he muttered. "Why do I have the feeling you had this all planned?"

George kept quiet, concentrating on keeping a straight face.

Finally Major Holt leaned forward, shook his head again and asked, "Just where is it you want to be transferred, Pvt. Lewis?"

"First Cavalry Division, Fort Bliss, Texas, Sir."

FT. BLISS, TEXAS
June 1942 to July 1943

It was almost noon when the train pulled into the El Paso station. The sun had had six hours to work its will on the desert and the heat rose up in a smothering cloud of dust that hit George in the face when he stepped off the train. About half the crowd milling about the platform was in uniform. Most of them, like George, carried large olive-drab duffel bags balanced on their shoulders. He found the bus transporting troops to Ft. Bliss and took a seat about half way back by a window. He looked at all the sand and tumbleweed and experienced a sudden nostalgic homesickness for the lush green coolness of the Upper Michigan woodlands.

The Franklin Mountains sloped up from the desert floor, dominating the landscape. Between them and the mountain range in Mexico, George knew, was the Rio Grande river and El Paso del Norte, the pass to the north, for which the city was named.

George studied the mountains, wondering if they were red rock like the ones Zane Grey described in the book he was reading. "What color would you say those mountains are?" he asked the young soldier in the seat next to him.

The boy was younger than George, probably just out of high school. He had red hair and a freckled face. George assumed the hair color from the freckles. One of his brothers had the same coloring. The boy bent down to peer out the bus window at the mountains. "Muddy brown", he answered. "You never seen mountains before?"

I'm from a place called Iron Mountain," George said, "but only the iron part is true. The mountain is mostly underground, in the mines."

"You a miner?"

"Nah. I did a little of anything I could find during the depression, but never mining. I'm George Lewis. Michigan and Wisconsin are my home turf."

The freckled youth extended an equally freckled hand. "Tim Jones, Wyoming," he said.

"Now there's a place I'd like to go," George said. "What part of Wyoming?"

The bus entered the post at the Pleasant View gate and drove past several adobe buildings with tiled roofs and arched porches before pulling up beside the central processing station. It was old and boxy, more like he expected to see on a military base. George noticed the worn shingles on the roof. He had had enough experience with roofing to see that it needed replacing and would probably leak if it ever rained here.

While waiting to be processed in he sat next to young Tim Jones and continued their conversation. George learned that Tim was from near Laramie. He liked mountain climbing and told George about shooting a mountain lion just before

Thanksgiving. "Me and my dad were out hunting when they hit Pearl," he said. "Where were you?"

"Sorting through old photographs with my girl," George said. "At her house."

After Jones was called, George finished the second Zane Grey book he'd bought in Junction City, *Shadow on the Trail*.

When they called him, he signed in and followed the guide to a small interview room. A Cpl. Reese held his travel orders.

"Do you have the rest of your orders with you."

George handed him an envelope.

The corporal shuffled through the papers, matching the serial numbers with the travel orders that had been handed to the driver as he got off the bus. He looked up at George inquiringly and then handed him off to the master sergeant.

The sergeant looked at the orders and said, "Lewis, follow me."

George followed him down the hall, further into the bowels of the building, wondering what was going on. They stopped in front of an office with a closed door and a frosted glass window. "Wait here," the sergeant said as he went in and closed the door.

It wasn't long before the door re-opened and George was ushered in to meet Capt. Penfold. George came to attention, saluted and said "Pvt. George Lewis reporting, Sir."

"At ease," the captain responded. George went into a military at ease pose, hands folded behind his back, feet spread, but still straight backed.

Capt. Penfold picked up a thin stiletto and slit open a second envelope from within the larger travel order envelope. George saw that it was addressed to the "Officer in Charge." Penfold extracted the single thin sheet and tipped back in his chair to read. Then he picked up the rest of the file and read it. Finally he looked up at the man standing in front of him.

"So," he said slowly. "Apparently you read regulations well. Not typical for an enlistee. You engineered a transfer out of a job you didn't like and asked to be sent here to Ft. Bliss."

"Yes, Sir."

Why?"

"I wanted to be with the horses, Sir,"

Capt. Penfold tipped back in his chair with his hands behind his head. George sensed a grudging respect from the man.

"Your skill at manipulating the rules has gotten you where you wanted to be. You do realize that this will be on your record for a long time and will hurt you when the opportunity comes for another promotion, don't you?"

"Yes, Sir, I understand that. But I didn't enlist to gain any such glory, Sir. I just enlisted to do my part to defend my country. If I do my part as a private or at a higher rank makes no difference to me."

"What if I put you to work drilling troops again?"

George's lower lip curled over his teeth and he bite it lightly. That hadn't occurred to him. He wet his lips with his tongue and then replied.

"I had hoped to be regular army and ship out after training, Sir."

The captain put the letter in his top drawer instead of back into George's file and tipped his chair back again. "OK, private, I'll grant your wish. We are set up here to fulfill the requests of each company and in doing so we have to take those requests by turn. Company C, 1st Brigade, 12th Regiment of the 1st Cavalry is requesting riflemen today."

Penfold hesitated a moment. "I hate to send you there, because of your record, but I have no choice. The first sergeant is a mean old dog from way back. He's rough, tough, and makes no bones about the fact that his word is law. You will do well to keep this in mind. Don't try to cross him, or your next trip to the guard house could last a very long time."

The master sergeant was called back and told to send George to Sergeant Grasman. The captain stood, they exchanged salutes. "Good bye, Private Lewis, and God speed in your eagerness to help in the war effort."

The top kick was as rough looking as Captain Penfold had said. He was an older guy, probably served in WWI. He had a jagged scar on his face that started at the corner of his right eyelid and ran across his cheek. It just missed the corner of his mouth and was lost to view under the collar of his spotless tan shirt. He looked the man standing in front of him up and down and finally said, "At ease, private"

The sergeant glanced quickly through the file. He picked up on the court-martial right away, stiffened and looked up at George, his gray-blue eyes flashing an inquisitive look. "Trouble maker, huh?" he said quietly.

George thought Grasman was talking to himself and didn't reply.

"Are you a trouble maker, soldier?" Grasman shouted.

"No Sergeant," George stammered. "I mean, only that one incident."

"If you're not a trouble maker, why were you transferred?"

"I requested it, First Sergeant." He thought from the tone of the conversation it might be wise to use the man's full title.

"Why'd you request transfer?" Grasman barked.

"I like horses, and wanted to serve with an outfit that would see combat. Didn't want to spend the whole war drilling troops."

Grasman ran his forefinger down the scar on his cheek. Then he stood and leaned forward, his hands on the desk. He wasn't much taller than the soldier in front of him. "I'll give you the benefit of the doubt, Lewis. I try to be a fair man, but I won't tolerate any trouble from you. When I give an order I expect it to be obeyed without question. It that clear?"

"Yes, Sergeant," George replied quickly.

Grasman raised his voice and summoned a corporal. "Cpl. Whitmore, show Pvt. Lewis how to find his quarters. He'll be filling one of the rifleman positions in troop C under Platoon Sgt. Draper."

George found the barracks easily. He was assigned to building 5B. The group of five three-story adobe buildings, with tiled roofs and sun porches on the second level, looked more like upscale apartment buildings than military barracks. He'd read in the pamphlet at HQ that the new buildings on post were WPA projects. They even had linoleum on the floors, a point the pamphlet writer seemed very proud of. There was a reading room on the first floor, something he'd never seen in a barracks before. The second floor had three rooms. The room he entered had 24 bunks; 48 men. That meant there were 144 men housed in Barracks 5B; the entire Company. There were five buildings in the group, therefore five companies, an entire battalion.

From the smell, George knew the stables must be close by. He found an empty lower bunk and stowed his gear in the footlocker. He located the showers and latrine down the hall and then he lay down, looked up at the bunk over him and replayed the last 48 hours in his mind. He felt a certain pride for engineering the transfer out of Ft. Riley and the hated job of D.I. That Capt. Penfold seemed nice. He wondered who'd written the letter, the major or Sgt. Blake? He also wondered what it said. He'd write a letter home after evening chow and tell Dad he had gotten into a combat unit at last.

That top sergeant, Grasman, reminded him of Parker, his high school math teacher. Just like Parker, Grasman had labeled him a troublemaker before he even had a chance to prove himself. Parker had picked on him because Donald, his older brother, had been in hot water more often than not. Now Grasman looked at George's coup de grace and transfer as proof he was a troublemaker.

I'm where I want to be now, he thought. I'll prove to him I'm not a troublemaker. He said he was a fair man, let's see if he is.

George had just drifted off to sleep when he was jolted back to consciousness by someone calling his name.

"Lewis, hey, son-of-a-gun, we're in the same outfit?"

It was Tim Jones. George swung his feet around and sat on the edge of his bunk. He automatically reached for a cigarette and lit it before answering. "Looks that way," he offered Tim a smoke.

Until the company was up to full strength, not much was happening. George and Tim spent the evening wandering around the base, getting acquainted, establishing landmarks. The mountains were the main feature, they and the water tower that overlooked the barracks.

The stables were just across the road from the barracks. They were fine brick buildings, as nice as the men's housing. There were 11 of them, each of which housed 112 horses or mules.

The men were restricted from entering the stables, which chaffed George somewhat. He was anxious to get a horse, it was the reason he'd chosen the cavalry. They saw Sgt. Grasman ride by on a rangy bay with a narrow blaze down her wide nose, a nice looking horse. He nodded at the two soldiers lounging in the shade of the water tower, but didn't speak.

The next day was still free time. George found the library in the basement of the administration building. He pulled a copy of Cavalry Regulations from the shelf and started reading. As always, what he read was indelibly imprinted in his mind. He'd been reading about an hour when an attention getting throat clearing made him look up. Instantly he was on his feet, saluting the captain.

"At ease, private," the man said. "Sit down. I'm Capt. Grant Kelly, Commanding Officer of Charlie Company. I noticed you're reading the regulations. Not the usual fare for a private."

"Oh, this," George said, tossing the book carelessly on the table. "I just like to know what's expected of me, Sir."

"You wouldn't by any chance be the young soldier who just transferred here from Ft. Riley, would you?" the Captain asked.

"Matter of fact, I did come from Ft. Riley, Sir," George said.

"Following a court-martial...a cleverly engineered court-martial?"

George grinned. "Well, you might say that, Sir. I tried every straight way I could to get into a combat unit, but they wouldn't listen to me."

"Do you write as well as you read, son?" asked the captain.

George shook his head, "I've never tried writing, Sir, except for letters home."

"We have a Division newspaper... what's the name, Lewis?

George nodded.

"We have a newspaper, Pvt. Lewis. I think you should get involved in it. Report to 2nd Lt. McCutcheon in the Headquarters building. Tell him I sent you."

"Is that an order, Sir?"

Capt. Kelly smiled and stood, motioning that George should remain seated. "No, Lewis, not an order, just a suggestion."

"Thank you, Sir," George answered, getting to his feet anyway. "I just may do that."

The third night there, George and Tim Jones ambled over to the enlisted men's club to shoot pool. They were sitting at a table with several others, watching the play and exchanging stories, when somebody clapped a hand on the back of

George's neck and said, "Jiggs Lewis, you son-of-a-woodtick. What the hell you doing here?"

George knew before he turned who it was. "Farley!"

George stood up and the newcomer caught him in a bear hug. Jack Farley stood six feet tall and he had a long reach. His hard-muscled forearms were covered with coarse golden hair. He picked George a couple inches off the floor and bounced him up and down a couple of times before he let him go.

"Holy Socks," George said. "It's good to see somebody from home. This is Jack 'Tinker' Farley" George introduced him to the crowd around the table. "We called him that back in Wisconsin because this man can make anything with an engine run, especially motorcycles."

Farley laughed and tipped his chin back to show the small scar on his jaw. "Wasn't able to get the ol' Harley running again after I slid on the ice and tangled with a hemlock tree," he said as he took a seat and put his long legs up on the table. "'Course this scar don't look like much now, but practically my whole brain was hanging outta there when they brought me in. Broke both arms and my leg too." Farley liked to embroider tales, and George was always his willing accomplice. The other guys at the table listened to him describe the black ice, and the way the load of snow on the branches of the hemlock tree covered him so thoroughly that he wasn't found for two days.

"I think you're a damned liar," drawled a pudgy fellow across the table. His voice was high pitched and his face had an ugly crop of pimples. It was Cpl. Whitmore, whom the men would soon learn was Grasman's stooge. He was an Oklahoma fella, a rancher or something like that.

"I beg your pardon, I didn't catch your name," Farley mocked the corporal's drawl, high pitch and all.

"Duane Whitmore, and I said I didn't believe your story."

Farley swept his eyes around the table gauging how the rest of the boys were taking this. Sensing the tide was with him, he drawled again, "What the hell's that got to do with it, Duane?" The way he said "Duane" made it clear he thought the guy was a sissy.

Some of the guys laughed and Whitmore pushed back from the table, his chubby face flushed red. "It's Cpl. Duane Dudley Whitmore, Private, and I'll thank you to remember that."

Farley tipped his head in acknowledgment and replied without the affected drawl. "OK Cpl. DeeDee Whitmore, I'll remember you." He leaned forward and scribbled DeeDee on a napkin and pushed it into the center of the table for everyone to see. All the guys roared and from then on Cpl. Whitmore would be DeeDee. Whitmore huffed off, leaving no one the sorrier.

Farley punched a mock fist into George's arm. "You ever get your bike back from Donald?"

George laughed and shook his head. His brother Donald had taken the cycle one night and wrecked it. "Never saw the money either. After that first ten dollars Dad made him cough up, he managed to avoid me every time I came home. Besides, after I joined the ticks and you got laid up, there wasn't much reason to own one. You know I couldn't keep it running without you around to tinker with it."

"Ticks," Jones said. "What the hell is that?"

"You ever heard of the CCC's?" George asked. "Up in Michigan we worked planting trees and we called ourselves woodticks. Ticks for short."

Farley and George entertained the younger men at the table, swapping stories about the days they'd worked together on Swede's farm in Wisconsin, and then about their year on the rails, living in the hobo jungles between Chicago and Milwaukee.

"What outfit they put you with?" George finally asked.

"The 12th Cavalry, Charlie Company," he said. "I've got to report to a Sgt. Grasman in the morning."

"Holy Socks! That's the unit I'm in. Can you beat that? Jones here, is in our outfit too."

"What's the top kick like? The man at headquarters said he was tough."

"Grasman? He's got a scar down the side of his face makes yours looks like a kitten scratch. Haven't seen him much, but I hear he's a stickler for having you jump when he says jump."

By the time the club closed, Farley and Jones were feeling no pain. George wasn't much of a drinker, more than a beer or two made him queasy.

They started back to the barracks. Between the enlisted men's club and the barracks was the Replica Museum. It was out-of-bounds after hours.

"Hey, what's this?" Farley shouted. "Looks like a cowboys and Indians fort."

"It's a museum, Old Ft. Bliss," George said. "Interesting place to look around."

"Then let's do it," Farley said, staggering into a closed gate. He jiggled the door knob. "Damn thing's locked." he said.

"It's after hours," George said. "We'll see it tomorrow."

Farley kicked at the gate. "Want to see it now. How 'bout you Jones? You want to see it?"

"Sure, I'll help you open that friggin' door," Jones said, his words slurred. He started toward Farley and stumbled over a stone set along the walkway, lost his balance, and fell sprawled across the path. George tried to pick him up, but in Jones' drunken state, it was like picking up a rail-road tie.

"Help me, Tinker," he said. Just then they heard the sound of horse's hooves coming from behind them. Glancing over his shoulder, George recognized the horse and its rider.

"Judas Priest, it's Grasman. Jones, get on your feet."

"Trouble here men?" Grasman called.

"No, Sergeant," George said. "This guy stumbled over one of the stones here is all."

"This area is out-of-bounds after dark, men." He rode closer. "Pvts. Jones and Lewis and someone I don't know." He slapped the leather riding crop he carried across his gloved hand. The sound cracked loudly though the courtyard and Jones finally struggled to his feet. "A known troublemaker and two accomplices," he said quietly, as if to himself, but loud enough to be heard. From his previous interview, George had learned these mutterings should be acknowledged.

"Yes, Sir."

Then Grasman's voice became hard, "Get back to your barracks. Now! That's an order."

Holding Jones upright between them, George and Farley headed for the barracks as fast as they could. "That's the second time he's called me a troublemaker," George told Farley. "And I haven't done anything wrong yet."

The bunk above George finally had someone in it. In the morning George introduced himself. His bunkmate was exceedingly skinny and had large ears which stuck far out from his head. His face was long and as thin as his body. George knew right away the kid was going to have a rough time fitting in.

Brad Liska was from New York City, he said. He had an accent George hadn't heard before. "Come to breakfast with us," George invited. "This is Tim Jones, Wyoming, and Tinker Farley, Wisconsin."

FT. BLISS – TWO

Harry Grasman was the most senior non-com officer at Ft. Bliss. The Cavalry had been his life since he joined up near the end of World War I. That's where he'd gotten the scar that jagged from the outer edge of his right eyebrow, down the side of his face and neck and ended somewhere under his spotless tan shirt. He was on his third cup of coffee, working on duty rosters for the upcoming week. The company was finally at full strength and training would start tomorrow morning.

A loud snore broke the silence in the cramped office. Grasman peered around the side of the desk and kicked the wooden box in which his black Labrador Retriever lay sleeping.

"Wake up, Snout, you're snoring again."

The dog raised his large head, looked up at his master and lay back down.

Grasman looked at the dog for a moment and then kicked the box again. "Come on, Snout, you need some exercise."

This time Snout roused himself out of the bed and came to stand beside his master's chair. Grasman opened a drawer, took out a stiff brush and began to brush the dog from head to tail. When he was done, he patted the dog on the head and reached for his own hat. "Let's go."

Grasman turned toward the mountains on Pleasant View Drive. The Sunday church goers had cleared out of the streets now and he could smell the scent of dinners coming from the row of officer's houses along the street. He approved of church going, but didn't do it himself. He liked the moral rules, the way he liked all rules, since they kept order in the world. God, he wasn't sure about. He didn't hold with begging God for things as if He were Santa Claus. God, he had often thought, was like Hairball, his cat. Loving when He felt like it, supremely independent at all times, and like as not to scratch you for no reason.

Like all the non-com officers, Grasman lived in one of the small red brick houses at the head of Howze Stadium. As he walked, he thought of what he'd fix for dinner. The mess hall held little appeal on weekends, especially when it was full of new recruits as it would be now. He stopped at the house next to his to see Jim Draper, his friend and fellow non-com. Maybe they'd ask him to eat with them. Draper's wife was a good cook.

Mrs. Draper came to the door when he tapped it gently with his riding crop. She was a mousy looking woman, somewhat plump. Her hair always looked like she couldn't get a comb through it, so she'd given up. She stood there, wiping her hands on the red gingham apron she wore over a yellow print dress. Harry was disappointed he couldn't smell anything cooking.

"Hi, Harry," she said. "It's Harry," she called over her shoulder. "Come on in. Jim isn't feeling too well today."

Inside the small living room, Sgt. Jim Draper sat in an overstuffed chair with his feet up on a foot stool, the Sunday paper draped over his lap. His complexion, even under the unshaved morning beard, was sallow. He still wore his gray bathrobe and worn slippers. Grasman thought he looked even worse than he had the last couple of weeks.

Grasman sat down on the sagging couch; Snout lay down at his feet. After the required niceties, he launched right into the reason for his visit.

"Looking over the records of the new men we got in, I see our company picked up a man who was a D.I. at Ft. Riley. He got into some sort of trouble and was court martialed and for some reason transferred here. He's an older guy, late twenty's. He's in your squad."

Draper pushed the newspaper off his lap and reached for a sheaf of paper on the coffee table next to him. He flipped the pages until he found the one he was looking for.

"George W. Lewis?"

"Yeah, that's the one. I figure he can handle your marching drills 'til you get feeling better. What'd ya think?"

"I haven't met him yet," Draper said. "What's he like?"

"Well, he's a little guy, but he wears his uniform with real authority. Since he's older, the younger men wouldn't resent him."

"What about the court-martial?"

"Capt. Kelly says he's clever. Says he engineered the court-martial just to get transferred to the Cavalry."

"What do you think?"

"Well, I kind of like the guy. But sometimes clever also means trouble. I ran into him and two other guys last night. The other two were drunk, but Lewis seemed to be trying to keep them in line. He may be a man to encourage, or a man to break, depending on what we see over the next few months." He rolled Snout's ears around then looked into the dog's face as if it were the dog he was talking to and not a fellow sergeant. "What do you think, Jim? Shall I put him on D.I. duty for you?"

That settled, Harry Grasman took Snout home, ate three ham sandwiches and some coleslaw and changed his clothes. He had a Polo Match at 1500 hours.

FT. BLISS - THREE

The duty roster posted on the bulletin board said George was to report to Platoon Sgt. Draper. The sergeant's skin was pale and he looked like he'd been ill. He cleared his throat every sentence or two when he talked.

"Lewis, Sgt. Grasman tells me you were attached to the recruit instructors at Ft. Riley as a drill instructor. My health is interfering with my duties some and I want you to take over the morning drill for me."

George hid his disappointment. But, after all, he reasoned, it wouldn't be forever like the job at Ft. Riley was. "Sure, Sarge." he answered. "When shall I start?"

George was drilling his 45 man squad the next afternoon when he spotted Grasman watching from the edge of the field. Time to show off. He began putting the men through their drill. He called "About - -face", pivoting the men 180 degrees, then marched them five paces and gave a "Present - - arms." When he gave the "Dress right - - dress," each man put his right hand on his hip, turned his head to the left so as to sight down the line and adjusted himself slightly to form a straight line. Suddenly Grasman came up beside George and bellowed out, "About -- face" and when the men had completed the maneuver he commanded, "At ease."

He lowered his voice and said, "Pvt. Lewis, what are you doing behind the squad? You can't drill troops from the rear."

"I sure can," George said. "This way it's much easier to apply a boot to their back sides if needed."

"Well, I've never seen it done that way, but if it works for you, carry on." He left, but George was aware of him watching the unusual drill technique almost every morning. George continued to drill from behind his squad, as he had at Ft. Riley.

Finally the Charlie company men were introduced to their horses and began training with them. George's horse was a strawberry roan, a gelding, as most of the horses were, and his name was Irish.

One morning orders were to prepare for an overnight training exercise in the desert. They took the horses, but weren't allowed to ride them for more than a mile outside post. George walked alongside Irish in the hot sun, pretending he was Wade Holden from Zane Grey's *Shadow on The Trail*. One of the descriptions from that book fit what he was seeing exactly, "the real Texas spread away to infinitude, gray and vast, a rolling barren of sagebrush." As they pushed through the sage, George pulled a handful of the dry needles and rubbed them between his hands. A pleasing, pungent smell filled his nostrils. Besides the sage there were hundreds of spiky plants with single tall stems as tall as the horses. Jones said they were yuccas.

They bivouacked in mid-afternoon near a stand of cottonwood trees where there was water for the horses. It smelled rank to George, but the horses drank eagerly. The horses had to be taken care of before the men could do anything else. Sgt. Grasman had made it quite clear that a man could be court-martialed for not taking proper care of his horse.

After the horses had been taken care of, the men pitched tents along non-existent streets. Their fronts had to form a perfectly straight line to the center of the tent town, where the command tents were. Sgt. Grasman's tent was at the head of the street George and Farley were assigned to. Cpl. Whitmore had his tent already pitched between Farley's and Grasman's and stood in front of it watching the rest of the men.

Farley and George worked next to each other pitching their tents when Farley looked up and saw the corporal watching him. He winked at George to let him know something was up.

"DeeDee," Farley called. "I'm having trouble making my tent stand up. Could ya come over here and give me some advice?"

Whitmore swaggered over. He examined the small one man tent and said he saw nothing wrong with it.

"No, it's twisted somehow," Farley insisted. "Look at it from inside."

As soon as DeeDee was three quarters of the way in the tent, Farley bumped the center post and the whole thing came down on top of the corporal. DeeDee started yelling and thrashing around and before Farley could free him, Grasman came running over.

"Private, get that tent off that man, NOW. That's an order."

"I'm trying, Sarge, honest I am."

What he was trying was to keep from laughing. "Be still, DeeDee, you're workin' against me," he yelled to the struggling man.

Grasman grabbed the tent and yanked it off his corporal. Cpl. Whitmore leapt to his feet, his eyes glaring. His normally ruddy complexion was flaming red, and sweat, or maybe it was tears, ran down his face. Pvt. Farley nonchalantly re-pitched the tent while Grasman stood and yelled at him.

"Soldier, that was a deliberate act and I will not tolerate horseplay in my outfit. You are on report."

While Farley had gotten himself in sideways with the top kick, George managed to get on his good side that evening when the men were ordered to practice some survival skills.

Each man was given one potato, two slices of bacon, two eggs, a slice of bread, dry coffee, and a canteen of water. Each was to work alone and prepare a meal for himself. As the men worked, the officers moved around observing.

Some of the men had rip-roaring fires going right away and tried to cook over the leaping flames. George dug a small pit, put a few desert stones in it, and added the dry mesquite he'd gathered from the desert a little at a time until he had a nice bed of coals. Then he peeled his potato and sliced it up. His tin cup sat on a hot rock and heated water for coffee while he fried the bacon over a low flame to make grease for the potatoes. Grasman and Capt. Kelly strolled by just as he was removing the bacon.

"That looks like an appetizing meal, private," the captain said. "Would you mind sharing a taste?"

"Sure thing, Sir" George said. "But it's not quite ready yet. If you'll wait a minute." The captain nodded and asked where he'd learn to cook over an open fire.

"I stayed many a night in the Hobo jungles during the deep depression," George told him, "Every scrap of edible food is precious, so you learn to do it right. Would you like toast, or just plain bread?"

"Toast would be nice," he answered as he turned to Sgt. Grasman. "Get your men around here, I want them to see how a field meal should be prepared."

As Capt. Kelly ate, he asked George if he'd been to see Lt. McCutcheon yet.

"No, Sir, I haven't had time," George answered.

"The methods you've used for preparing this fine meal would make a great article, Private. I wish you'd write it up and take it to McCutcheon to prove you have something to say."

"Is it an order this time?" George asked. He was grinning as he divided the rest of the coffee between his cup and the captain's.

"No, just a strong suggestion," the captain answered.

George, along with Farley and Tim Jones, made a trip across the border to Juarez the first time they could get passes. Farley wanted to see the bull fights. George left when the picadors began to place their decorated pics into the neck muscles of the bulls to weaken them. While everyone shouted "Ole", George stood outside and smoked a couple of cigarettes.

"What'd you leave for," Jones asked when they found him after the fight.

"I don't think it's much sport to fight a wounded animal," George said.

"I knew we should've come without you," Farley said. To Jones he confided, "Jiggs has a soft spot for animals, can't stand to see them hurt."

George didn't defend himself; it was true. It had angered him to see animals neglected and starving during the depression, and even when food was scare he'd feed a little to the stray dog or cat he'd come across. To deliberately hurt an animal for sport was too much.

"You hunt deer," Jones said.

"Only for meat," George replied. "I never killed anything for sport."

FT. BLISS - FOUR

At Wednesday's mail call George received a letter from Patsy, his fiancée. Patsy wrote mushy letters, full of sexy stuff so George stuck it in his back pocket and waited until evening when he could read it privately in his bunk. It was dated a full week before and as soon as he saw the greeting he knew that something was wrong. She always started "Dear Honey Pie,: but this letter read,

> *Dear Jiggs,*
> *I don't know just how to say this, and I hate to let you down just before you ship out, but there's no use pretending either. I've met someone else and I want to break our engagement. You don't know him, I met him in Escanaba where I am working now. We had some good times and I'll always remember you. Please don't write anymore. I'm sorry.*
> > *Sincerely,*
> > Patsy

He read it again trying to make it say something different, but no matter how the words were twisted, it came out Dear John. George balled up the pale blue sheet and tossed it in the air. It hit the bunk overhead and rebounded. He played an absent-minded game of catch with it while his mind reviewed his three-year courtship with Patsy.

George and Frank Goodwin, Patsy's older brother, had been in the CCC camp together. Camp Cooks was only seven miles from the Goodwin farm, but almost 200 miles from Iron Mountain. George didn't get to go home very often, so Frank took him home with him whenever they could both get weekend passes at the same time. At first Patsy was just a pesky high school student, but after a while, George looked forward to seeing her.

She wasn't pretty, but she was always laughing, showing her white even teeth in an open smile. She was fun to be with. George remembered the time they'd stopped at Paul's Corner Bar and he'd played the punch board at two bits a punch to win her a pair of real silk hose. Patsy had danced around and gotten so excited she planted a big kiss on his mouth right there in front of everybody. *'That was worth the week's pay I blew to win them for her.'*

One memory after another came up as he lay in his bunk. After taps Farley came in, weaving a little from drinking, but Farley wasn't the one to talk to about heartbreak. It was against regulations to be in the stables after dark, but Irish was the only one George trusted with deep feelings.

Getting into the stables was easy. After the sentry passed the door, he just walked in. The warm spicy smell of the horses mingled with straw accosted his nose. Several of the horses nickered softly. George found his way to Irish's stall and clicked his tongue to greet him. Irish nudged George, looking for a carrot or a lump of sugar.

"Sorry, Pal, there isn't any. This is an unplanned trip." He puttered around, currying the horse's coat and checking his feet while he talked out loud about Patsy.

"I'm not sure I was in love with her, Irish. We had some good times together, but I don't think I'm feeling bad about her, just bad about being jilted. Anyway, she couldn't have loved me. Hell, it's only been ten months. Who is there left up there for her anyway? Draft dodgers and cowards that won't sign up, that's who." Irish shook his head and swished his tail against a fly. "Well, of course, there may be someone else who is just color blind like me and they screened him out."

He threw the lightweight fly sheet over her back, snapped it in place, and sat down on a bale of hay to reminisce some more about his lost lady. He was about to get up and go outside to light up a Lucky when he heard someone come in. Whoever it was stopped two stalls up. It had to be Grasman. That's where his horse, Dolly, was stabled. George kept quiet hoping he wouldn't be discovered and listened to the Sergeant talk to his horse the way George had been talking to Irish.

"Ah, Dolly, my love," he spoke softly, as if to a woman, "What a beauty you are, gentle but full of fire. You remind me of old Duke. Did I ever tell you how old Duke carried me back to the line when I was wounded in the Argonne?

The horse nickered as if in reply.

"Yes, of course I have," he chuckled deep in his throat. "You're probably sick of hearing about it."

The sounds of him working, probably sweeping the rubber currycomb across her from shoulder to flank filled the quiet stables. Now and then another horse would neigh softly, or shift position. Other than that, it was dead quiet. It was unusual to have a mare in the cavalry. They were often ill-tempered. Likewise there were no stallions, only geldings who were gentle and not distracted by the things the mares and stallions were. George wondered why Grasman was allowed to keep Dolly. She was a beauty, a reddish bay with a narrow blaze down her wide nose.

"Well now, Dolly, let's check those feet." He was moving around her, lifting each foot checking for small cracks or stones he might have missed in her normal grooming. "We're deep in it now, Dolly," he told her, "it'll be combat again pretty soon. I've got a fine troop of men to go with, soon as they're whipped into top form. You'll see, we'll show those Nips and Krauts what Americans are made of."

George had been holding back a cough for five minutes, repeatedly creating and swallowing excess saliva to soothe the tickle when, without warning, he sneezed.

Instantly Grasman ran into the corridor. "Who goes there?" he shouted.

No use trying to hide, he'd be found anyway and then it'd go worse for him.

"Pvt. Lewis here," he said, stepping out of the stall.

"What are you doing here?" the sergeant barked.

After what he'd heard George knew how he felt about his horse, so he made a play for sympathy.

"I couldn't sleep, Sarge. Sometimes I just miss everybody at home so much and Irish is the only one I can talk to. I was just about to leave when I heard you come in. Sorry, I won't do it again."

Grasman stood with his muscles tensed like a wrestler outside the stall entrance. He was out of uniform, wearing a pair of swim trunks, an olive drab tee shirt with a rip under one arm, and sandals on his feet. *Holy cow, I'll be on KP for a month along with Farley.* George thought.

"Guess that's why I come too," Grasman said. George relaxed.

"I've had this horse eight years and she's my best friend." He moved along side George and patted him on the back, guiding him toward the door. Once outside, he stopped, offered a cigarette and they stood and smoked together.

The moon was just a pale sliver over Sugar Loaf Peak and there were a jillion stars. Grasman told him the whole story of old Duke saving him in World War I.

"I was only nineteen," he said. "A mine exploded next to us and the shrapnel flew, slicing open my face like a filet from a fish's rib. Just missed the juggler here," he pointed to his neck where the narrow scar passed close to the large artery. "Duke took me back to the medics and I didn't die. Just ended up ugly for life. Dolly is his direct descendant. Trained her myself."

"I wondered about her being a mare," George said, "since all the rest of the animals are geldings."

"Dolly's special," Grasman said.

They finished their smokes and Grasman patted George on the back again. "Go to bed, son, and don't let me catch you in here after hours again."

"No, Sarge," George said quietly, "thank you. G'night."

He walked back to the barracks, Patsy completely out of his mind for now. He'd written two articles for the camp newspaper so far, and he thought a profile of Sgt. Grasman would be interesting. He could interview him on the polo field and bring in some of the background he'd just learned. Maybe it would make the man seem more human to others.

Meanwhile the training with the horses went on.

"I feel like a character out of one of Zane Grey's books," George said to Jones as they waited their turn to charge the firing range targets at full gallop.

"When do we get to do some of that riding over the purple sage and fire at people chasing us?" Jones teased.

"Apparently that's not the kind of war they're sending us to," George replied. "I've been reading in the papers. The Germans and the Russians are going at each other with tanks on the Russian border. It would have been a cavalry battle fifty years ago. The Japs have been sneaking into the Aleutian Islands up by Alaska and they're fighting in New Guinea, just north of Australia. New Guinea probably isn't worth much, but they'd sure like to take Australia."

"You're especially keen to fight the Nips aren't you?" Jones asked.

"Well, the way I figure it, the Japs, or Nips as you call 'em, are our war. The European thing, we're just helping out. Yeah, given a choice, I'd rather go to the Pacific."

Jones thought a minute. "No, I figure both wars are ours. Haven't you read about the German sub they captured off the coast of Florida? They're gonna execute the six Germans as spies. Florida is closer than those Aleutians, or Australia."

"Just the same," George said. "I enlisted to fight the Japs and I'm hoping that's where they send us."

The horses and men trained daily. One of the drills they ran involved riding zigzag through bales of hay at faster and faster speeds. George and Irish became as one, and Irish's response to the slightest pressure of the leg to turn one direction or another was instantaneous. While racing across the sand on the back of his horse, George experienced a feeling of elation which he'd never had before.

After a few weeks of these drills, Grasman organized ride-and-shoot contests between companies each weekend. Each company fielded a team of five riders and the team with the fastest ride and most targets hit won a keg of beer from the other company. These weekend ride-and-shoot contests were like an enlisted man's Polo game. Grasman took an intense interest in both.

George ended up a regular rider for Grasman because he consistently hit the bulls eye on all six bales and Irish was a fast horse.

One Friday afternoon Grasman had the whole troop lined up in the hot sun delivering a lecture about taking care of the horses. They'd been standing in rank for about twenty minutes with Grasman pacing back and forth in front of them. Farley started turning his head from side to side to follow Grasman's movements as if he was watching a tennis ball bounce from court to court. Grasman turned suddenly and caught him.

"Pvt. Farley," he shouted. "Am I bothering you?"

"No Sarge," Farley replied promptly.

"Why are you jerking your head around?"

"I must have slept wrong. I have a crick in it."

"Ten laps ought to loosen it up, soldier. Now! That's an order."

"Ten laps in this heat doesn't seem fair," George whispered to the guy next to him.

Grasman turned like a savage bulldog. "Don't question me, soldier. When I give an order everyone obeys whether he thinks it's fair or not. Is that clear?"

"Yes, Sergeant," George replied as Grasman pointed with his swagger stick that he was to join Farley. Out of the corner of his eye he saw a smirk on Whitmore's face. He'd like to wipe that off. Towards Grasman, he felt no animosity, he was only doing his job. DeeDee Whitmore was another case.

FT. BLISS - FIVE

The following Saturday George arrived at the stables right after morning chow to get Irish ready for the ride-and-shoot contest. He greeted the horse by stroking his nose and letting him find the sugar cube held loosely in his hand.

After a few minutes of talking quietly to him, George pulled on his gloves and picked up the oval scrubber brush. He worked over the horse's coat to bring any dirt and loose hair to the surface. Irish seemed to especially like the soft brush George used next to brush away the debris loosened by the scrubber. George took the rough mitt and cleaned around the horse's eyes, then followed with a damp sponge around the eyes and velvet nostrils.

George combed the reddish blonde mane, then the long tail, working in a conditioner.

"Now the feet, boy," George said, picking up each foot and cleaning it with pick and brush before dressing the hoof. When he picked up the right fore foot and brushed, Irish winced.

"Whoa, fella," George said. "What's the problem?"

The problem was a tiny pebble no bigger than four grains of sand, buried deep in the tender frog area of the foot. George removed it, but Irish still refused to put his full weight on it. The pebble had evidently bruised the tender inner cup.

"Well, Irish, you can't run today, can you?" George stroked his nose and then finished the grooming by rubbing his coat with a soft cloth sprayed with alcohol. "I'll go tell Sarge. He'll probably put me on report for not finding that stone yesterday."

Grasman wasn't on the field yet, so George located Farley, Jones, and Brad and let them know he wasn't going to ride.

"Maybe you can fill in for me," he said to Jones. "You're fast even if you miss a target or two."

"Here comes Grasman," Farley said. "Let's go see what he says."

Grasman saw the four men walking towards him and advanced to meet them.

"Where's your horse, Lewis?" he asked. "You should be warming him up."

"Irish is lame, Sarge," George told him. "I can't ride today."

"You gotta ride, Lewis. The guys are counting on you winning the beer."

"But my horse is lame, Sarge," George repeated. "I can't ride a lame horse."

"Take my horse," he retorted. "You can ride Dolly."

George was surprised by this offer. Grasman had never let anyone else even groom Dolly, let alone ride her.

"I can't do that, Sarge."

"Why not?" he asked. The other team had arrived. Grasman waved at their company sergeant. "Hate that son o'bitch, Belch," he muttered under his breath.

Belch was a young man, tall, slim and handsome; everything Grasman wasn't. He sat astride a huge black horse whose coat gleamed in the sun. Grasman's horse was a hand shorter, but as powerful, and she had beaten Belch and his horse in numerous races.

"We only beat this team by one target last time, Lewis," Grasman said to him. "We can't afford to let our seconds, like Jones, for instance, ride against 'em." He dismounted and tried to hand Dolly's reins to George.

"Sarge," George said, backing off a bit and showing Grasman the palms of his hands as if to ward him off, "you know it's against regulations to make a man ride a strange horse except in an emergency."

"Damn it, man, we have to win the beer. I said ride my horse. Now take her, that's an order." He handed George the reins and Dolly was in George's hands.

"OK, Sarge" he said. There wasn't anything else he could say.

George approached Dolly from the near side and started talking to her. He stroked her neck as he walked beside her the hundred yard length of the field. At the far end he mounted her and rode back to where Grasman stood watching.

"She's a hand taller than Irish," he told him, "the stirrups are wrong for me. I'm going to walk her back to the stable and put my own saddle on her."

"There isn't time," Grasman said as he adjusted his stirrups to fit, "they'll be starting soon."

The breeze which had been blowing all morning picked up some, making dust devils in the dry loose dirt of the field. George mounted Dolly again and rode her at full gallop around the field. She was faster than Irish and ran more smoothly.

Dolly was feeling fresh and high like she really wanted to run. George put her through the corkscrew pattern, starting in a large circle until she took a breath and relaxed. Then he begin to screw her in, making smaller and smaller circles until they were turning in place. He reversed directions and unscrewed the pattern until the full wide circle was complete.

Farley and Jones had set up some hay bales so George could practice actually riding the turns. The critical thing in barrel racing and shooting is the control of the horse with your legs. The first run through George used audible signals, calling "here" at each turning point. Dolly's ears were up and back, so he knew she was listening. She picked up every cue. They rode it again, picking up speed. There was time for one more practice run. This time George used only the leg signals at each turn. George felt fairly comfortable with her and reached over to pat her neck.

"Good work, Dolly, looks like we're up. Let's go win the beer for your Old Man."

Just like bowling, you put your two best competitors at lead and anchor. George usually rode lead, but to give him more time to get used to Dolly, Grasman had switched him to last. Grasman came up to meet them. He patted Dolly's neck while he talked.

"We're two seconds ahead and two targets down, so you only gotta hit three out of five. Speed is what you need. Dolly's fast, let her run."

The men began to whoop and holler when George rode Dolly up to the line and waited until he felt ready to go. He was more nervous than usual. Glancing over to where the troop was clustered together, George could see Grasman standing at the front of them, the gloat of victory already evident in his grin and stance.

George pulled his .45 caliber Smith & Wesson from its holster, checked the load, and replaced it. The eight hay bales were lined up down the center of the field, twenty-five feet apart. The first and last bales had no targets. The ride up between the bales was where he'd pick up speed and then fire at the targets on the return. To fire at the targets the riders had to shift weight and swing the gun from side to side to hit the target first on the left and then the right. George signaled the timer he was ready and Dolly leapt forward with the starting gun. Man and horse wove in and out of the bales, reached the end at top speed and turned.

Pistol in hand, laying into the turns, George fired at the first target and missed. He heard the bullet bury itself in one of the barrier bales lining the course. The second and the third targets were dead center. He only needed one more.

He swung his body over to aim at the target on his right. Dolly turned to start her arc around the bale, but their timing was off. When George pulled the trigger it was Dolly's head in front of him instead of the target. The bullet went directly between her ears and deep into her brain. Her front legs crumpled and George went flying over her head. The hay bale he'd been shooting at cushioned his fall somewhat as he hit it with his right shoulder and rolled.

From his position on the ground George could hear the shouting and knew what had happened. He'd killed the Sergeant's horse!

Grasman was at her side before George could regain his feet, then he was over George screaming, shaking his fist, mostly incoherent with rage.

"You bastard, you god damn fucking idiot!"

George struggled to his feet and saw the horse laying on the ground, dark red blood still flowing from her head and soaking into the thirsty dust of the arena. He felt sick and felt the contents of his stomach rising. It reached his throat, burning with acid. He managed to choke it back down. Somebody thrust an open canteen into his hand and he drank gratefully. The side of his face stung and when he put a hand up to it, it came away wet with blood. His shirt sleeve was torn where his right shoulder had bit the dirt and blood oozed from a scrape there too. His legs were shaking.

"My god, Sarge, I'm sorry," he managed, but Grasman wasn't listening. His face was beet red, except for the scar which stayed deadly white, and he continued to scream and cuss.

Noticing the scar gave George something to focus on and he began to calm down. The pounding of his heart subsided and he drew in a deep breath, then let it out slowly. On the next breath he felt himself relax. He reached out to touch Grasman's arm, a reflex movement meant to comfort. Grasman shook it off.

"Don't touch me. You deliberately shot Dolly to get even with me. I'll have you court-martialed for this and hope they throw away the guardhouse key."

"Sarge," George shouted back, losing his temper, but still trying to maintain military respect, "It was an accident. I feel as bad as you do."

That was the wrong thing to say. Grasman lunged at George who put up his fists to defend himself. Cpl. Whitmore and Sgt. Draper grabbed Grasman from behind at the same time Jones stepped in front of George.

"Capt. Kelly coming," Farley hissed in his ear.

Grasman pulled free from his keepers and started for George again with a guttural snarl, his hands reaching for the throat. He hadn't seen the captain. Farley waited until Grasman was in motion before he yelled "Attention" as if he had just spotted the captain. Even then Grasman would have continued if Whitmore and Draper hadn't grabbed him again.

This time Kelly himself shouted "Attention" and everybody snapped to and saluted.

"Sgt. Grasman, what's going on here?" he asked.

"This dumb, stupid, son-o-bitch private just shot my horse, that's what." His voice quivered and he sucked at his inner cheek to stiffen his lip to keep from crying.

"Sergeant," Kelly spoke in a tone of command, "it appears to me you were about to strike this man. Get yourself under control."

He turned to address George. "Pvt. Lewis, what do you have to say?"

"When I told the sergeant my horse was lame and I couldn't ride. He ordered me, twice, to ride his horse."

"Had you ever ridden his horse before?" Kelly asked.

"No, Sir. I had ten, maybe fifteen minutes to get used to her before my ride. On the fifth target she turned too soon, and, well, it was a terrible accident."

The Captain turned again to Grasman. "What was Pvt. Lewis doing on your horse?"

"Sir," Grasman said his voice steady now, "Pvt. Lewis is a good rider and a good marksman, I saw no reason not to let him use my horse so we'd win the contest. But he shot her to get even for some discipline I administered yesterday that he thought was unfair. I want a court martial hearing against him."

Capt. Kelly shook his head. "You know as well I do that you issued an illegal order when you ordered a man to ride a strange horse in a non-emergency situation. I'm sure you won't be able to argue that winning a keg of beer was an emergency. I'm surprised Pvt. Lewis didn't inform you of the regulation. He knows regulations as well as any officer."

"He did, Sir." It was Jones speaking up even through he hadn't been addressed. "Those were his very words, but Sarge told him *we have to win the beer.*' Then he said it was an order."

The captain nodded. "It's a shame to lose such a beautiful animal, but it was an accident and I won't hear of any disciplinary measures being taken against Lewis. Unless, of course, you still want to press charges."

"You bet I do," Grasman replied. The look he gave George was filled with hatred.

"Then come to my office to file them." The captain gave a "fall out" order and turned to leave.

The crowd began to re-gather around Dolly. "Let's get out of here," Farley said, grabbing George's arm and urging him away.

But Grasman shouted. "Lewis, get a shovel and start digging Dolly's grave. The least you can do is give her a decent burial. And strip my gear off before you move her. That's an order, get moving."

Before there was any chance of reply, Kelly returned.

"Sgt. Grasman, I'm going to rescind that order. Call the engineers and have a bulldozer dig the grave." He pointed to three men. "Remove the gear and return it to the stables."

He turned to George, "You hurt yourself in that tumble, Pvt. Lewis?"

"Just a few bruises I think, Sir."

"Nevertheless, report to sick bay and have those wounds cleaned. Now; and that is an order." He said to one of his aides, "Take this man over to Beaumont. Have him report back to me when they've finished with him. Grasman, you come with me."

Kelly was doing most of the talking and Grasman was looking mighty uncomfortable as the two walked away. "I'd sure like to hear what he's saying to him," Farley said as he walked along with George.

FT. BLISS - SIX

Harry Grasman lay on the lumpy green sofa staring up at the ceiling fan. It rotated slowly. Did it have five arms or six? No matter, it did nothing to cool the stifling room. An empty Black Velvet bottle lay on its side next to the empty glass within arms reach. A large orange cat sat on his chest.

"Hairball," his voice was quavering. "She's gone, Hairball, gone."

The cat snuck close and rubbed its mouth along Grasman's jaw over and over, while Harry rubbed its ears. "I can't believe she's gone. One minute running like the wind, the next laying there, the life oozing out." He sobbed aloud then half sat up and blew his nose in an olive drab handkerchief. He laid back down.

"And that private...Lewis. I knew he was a troublemaker from the minute I laid eyes on him. I'll see him rot in hell, I swear."

He stared through his bleary eyes at the cat who had ceased rubbing against him and lay quietly on his chest looking at him through the narrow vertical slits of his eyes. "Yeah, I know," Grasman admitted to the cat. "But what can I do? That wimpy captain won't let me press charges." He was silent for a while and almost fell asleep, but suddenly sat up and lurched to his feet.

"There must be another bottle of whiskey here," he muttered to himself as he threw open one cupboard door after another. There wasn't. "Draper will have some," he assured himself as he reached for the door. Hairball got under his feet and he sent the cat to the other side of the room with one swift kick. "Keep the hell from under my feet, cat." he yelled as he slammed the door behind him.

Grasman and Draper sat in Draper's small living room, drinking Draper's whiskey. The room was decorated with chairs almost too small for a man. There were ruffles and frills everywhere. On top of that, the predominant color was pink. It always made Grasman feel sorry for Draper. Draper listened while Grasman talked.

"She was a great horse, Jimmy," he said, looking the full glass of whiskey right in the eye. "Hell of it is, Lewis was a great rider. Can't figure how he shot her."

"It really was an accident, Harry," Jim said. "A horrible accident.."

"I'm not convinced of that, Jim. Didn't I tell you at the first Lewis was clever? I said, and I quote, 'he'll either be a man to make or a man to break.' Well, I've decided. I'll break him."

He downed the amber liquid. It burned with a comforting warmth all the way down.

"Don't forget one thing," Jim Draper advised. "Kelly seems to have sort of adopted him. You press Lewis too hard you might get in sideways with the captain."

"I can be clever, too." Grasman said. "I'll stay within the rules, but I'll make his life miserable. He'll wish he'd stayed at Ft. Riley drilling troops."

William Beaumont, the El Paso hospital, was off-post, up in the foothills of the Franklin Mountains. George sat in the waiting room, his face in his hands. Farley sat beside him, his lanky frame hanging loose.

"Ah, come on, Jiggs. It wasn't your fault."

"Doesn't make me feel any better, Tinker. She was a great horse. Why'd he have to go and make me ride her?"

Farley sat back and stretched his long legs out in front of him. "Wonder what they did with the beer?"

"I'll bet the other side took it. They won, didn't they?"

"Nope, it was all tied up when you hit the horse, and it all came to an end right there. Wonder what they did with it?"

"When Grasman cools off, I'm going to get him to listen to me," George said. "I was going to write an article about him playing Polo and weave in the story he told me about his getting wounded in the Argonne Forest battle. Maybe I can do some sort of tribute to Dolly that would make him feel better."

"Don't count on it, buddy," Farley said. "I got him pegged as a guy who carries a grudge for a long time.

"Pvt. George Lewis," a nurse came to the door and called his name. George rose to follow her.

The nurse was young, not particularly good looking, but she smelled of soft powder and had a nice smile. She gently cleaned George's face, holding his chin in one hand while she worked on his cheek. "Bad scrape there," she said. "What happened?"

George told her and she clicked her tongue in sympathy. "I suppose the sergeant is real upset with you."

"That's an understatement," George said, wincing as she applied iodine to the scrape. "He's talking court-martial"

"Oh, I hope they don't do that," the nurse said. "Surely it was an accident?"

The nurse finished with the shoulder scrape, saying it wasn't as deep as the one on his face. "It'll be sore for a couple of days, but don't you baby it. Keep it moving."

She gave him some salve to apply to his wounds twice a day. George thought about asking her for a date, but considering he didn't know what the future held for him, he decided to postpone it. He got her name, Laura, thanked her, and returned to find Farley in the waiting room.

When George reported back to the captain, Kelly informed him there would be no charges filed. "But I'd stay out of Grasman's way for a few days," he cautioned.

Keeping out of Grasman's way was easier said than done since one of the main jobs of the first sergeant was to make out the duty roster. After the shooting of the horse, George became a regular on the bubble dancing circuit.

"The joke of it is, I don't mind KP." George told Farley and Jones as they played pool at the enlisted men's club. "The cook is a pleasant sort, being in the mess hall keeps me off the drill field in the hot sun, and I have access to plenty of between meal snacks of the first-class sort."

It was the third time in five days George spent the afternoon policing Noel field. The chirping of sparrows and the harsh grate of a blackbird kept him company. Grasman might not be able to court-martial him, but he was intent on sticking him with the worst duty he could.

He looked up at the mountains off and on. A dark stripe ran across the entire face of them, about half way up. George wondered how it came to be there, in an even line all the way across. Another stripe almost at the tallest peaks was lighter. He wondered again what color it really was, and how Zane Grey would describe it. He had become convinced Zane Grey exaggerated the glories of Texas. He sure hadn't seen any of those fantastic beautiful spots he'd written about. It was all just sand and rocks and cactus. And it was hotter 'n hell.

Farley hello'd from the porch of the barracks and held up a bottle motioning George in that direction. They met at the edge of the field and George drank the cold root beer with gratitude.

"The new duty roster has been posted and you aren't scheduled for any shit duties all the rest of the week."

"What happened?"

"Seems the captain caught the fact that your name came up twice as often as it should on KP and trash pick-up and I heard it from the cook that Grasman was forbidden to put you on those duties more than once a month."

But Grasman was not to be out done. He started coming up with new and different shit details for Pvt. Lewis. What's more, he began to include Farley when he perceived what close friends they were.

By this time, George had given up apologizing to Grasman and started to play the game the way Grasman set it up. It had become a post joke. George treated Grasman just the same as he had before, but Grasman tried to ignore the Private as much as he could

George and Farley got acquainted with Grasman's cat, Hairball, the day they were sent to pull weeds from the flower garden in front of his house. He wasn't growing cactus like a sensible man would in the desert, but had a bed of red & white petunia's bordered with yellow marigolds. The cat used the soft soil of the garden as a litter box. Farley ran into the evidence about the same time the cat appeared and started brushing up against George, flicking a fluffy orange tail in his nose.

"Get outta here." George said and pushed the cat aside. He was right back, rubbing his whiskers against George's knee, and purring. "How is it his animals all love me and he hates me?" He picked up the cat and tossed it twenty feet away.

"Wouldn't take much to wring his neck and bury him in here alongside his droppings," Farley observed.

"No," George said, "I can't hurt an innocent animal just for a come-uppance to Grasman. I've got a better idea."

They finished pulling the weeds just before lunch. After mess George went 'round to the kitchen and asked the cook for a cup of sugar. When he heard why George wanted it he laughed and gave him a couple pounds of it.

The two volunteer gardeners worked all of the cook's white fertilizer into the ground around the flowers and watered it in.

The following week George and Farley strolled past Grasman's house. Everything was dead. "Must be that cat manure he's been using," Farley said. They laughed.

When George met Grasman on his way to the mess hall he called out "Morning, Sarge. "Would you like me to weed your flowers this afternoon." Grasman just glowered and said "Never mind."

FT. BLISS - SEVEN

Grasman was already up and dressed when the bugler blew reveille at 0400. He could hear the steady drip of rain on his tent and knew the camp would be a quagmire of mud by now. Although he hated the dampness, everything was cold and clammy and his boots were still damp from yesterday, the mud would be a definite advantage to the cavalry. The entire 1st Cavalry Brigade was on maneuvers on the Texas-Louisiana border along the Sabine River. Their opponents were General Patton's sixth army, tank artillery. Grasman knew this was one of the most important training maneuvers he had ever participated in, for they were there to determine which army could out-maneuver the other, the horse-mounted cavalry or the mechanized army of Patton. It was a simple equation... if the cavalry lost they'd also lose the horses. He'd let his men know this, so they would approach the maneuvers with more enthusiasm than usual.

General William Chase was commanding. Grasman respected him, thought he was "full of pepper". The Cavalry bivouacked on the south end of the maneuvering ground while Patton's army assembled thirty, thirty five miles north of them.

Grasman stepped outside his tent and shivered. There was a dense fog which prevented him from seeing more than two tents beyond his own. He could hear Sergeant Draper coughing in the tent next to his. Jimmy shouldn't be here, Grasman thought. I'll bet he never ships out with us.

"Morning, Jimmy," he called. "You stay there, I'll be right back with some joe." He slogged through the mud to the mess tent and came back with two steaming cups of strong black coffee. The men were beginning to emerge as dark moving shadows from the two man tents they'd slept in. Harry watched with satisfaction as they headed first to the stables to see to their horses morning ration of oats. They had half an hour to get breakfast before the bugler blew formations. The exercises began at 0600 sharp.

The horses were housed better than the men. Grasman stood under the stable tent, a dry layer of hay under his feet and saddled his horse. The big roan was skittish. Grasman slapped his rump to get him to move so he could throw the saddle over his back. Dolly had almost saddled herself. Brute was stupid. Even the horse's name chaffed him.

He glanced around involuntarily for that bastard, Lewis, even though he knew he wasn't in the stable. Lewis was the gunner of Draper's seven-man machine gun squad and Grasman had seen him and his squad double checking everything when he walked to the stable to get Brute. Private Jones, number-four man in the squad and driver of the number-one pack mule, had nodded at him when he passed. It had seemed like a malicious nod. Grasman kept a suspicious eye on everyone Lewis was friendly with, especially Farley and Jones. One of the things he'd noticed was the respect Lewis got from the other men. It wasn't only because he was older than most of them; it was something else. Grasman tried to shake the animosity toward Lewis out of his head. He had to get over this. It wasn't good for the Company.

Umpires, identified by the white band they wore on their arms, swarmed around the camp like flies. During the exercise they would be determining casualties. A dead man would be tagged with black, a casualty still able to carry on, yellow, and a non-walking casualty, orange. There was no arguing with an umpire's decision.

The troop didn't go far the first day. Company C, with their accompanying umpires, moved east and followed the river bank north. At noon they stopped and ate K-rations in the drenching rain. The brick sized box, decorated with blue waves to indicate it held dinner and not breakfast or supper, contained a tin of Spam. Grasman opened his with the accompanying lead key. He mixed the dried broth package with the cold water in his canteen cup and drank it. Draper, obviously struggling to keep going, sat next to Grasman. His face was pale and his coughing fits frequent.

"Jimmy," Grasman said. "You better go back to base and report to sick bay. This damp ain't doing you any good and your coughing is likely to reveal our position in a tight spot."

Draper looked relieved. "Cpl. Whitmore will ride with you."

Grasman turned and called Whitmore.

"Put Lewis in charge of the squad," Draper said. "I know you don't like him, but he's the most capable." Grasman nodded. He knew it too. Besides, Lewis was the gunner and regulations put him in charge automatically when the squad leader was absent.

The next morning they could hear the rumbling of tanks in the distance. Lt. Hamilton, Charlie Company field commander, led his men around the sound where they hid in the bushes and watched Patton's soldiers try to move the tanks through the mud. The treads of the lead tank had disappeared and men were shoveling and pushing branches under the treads to try to get it moving. It'd been like that in Germany, Grasman thought. The army spent a lot of time and effort digging out the tanks while, like now, the horses stepped along, carrying the Cav behind the enemy. The entire Company passed unseen within a thousand yards of them. It would have been satisfying to engage the enemy then and there, but Capt. Kelly's orders were to capture Patton's headquarters.

The third morning, the rain stopped, the sun came out and the weather turned steamy hot. George's squad made contact with an enemy patrol just before noon. When the skirmish was over, the umpire put a yellow tag on Jones's right arm to indicate he was wounded. His mule had a black tag, so the men had to redistribute its packs to the other three mules and off load some of the ammo to the horses. They'd wiped out the enemy patrol.

Normally Grasman would have commended the squad who made the first kill, but he'd be damned if Lewis would hear praise from him. Suddenly he remembered the night he'd caught Lewis in the stables and how he'd felt drawn to the younger man. If Dolly hadn't been shot... Grasman turned away; angry with Lewis, Draper, and the whole damn system.

Soon after that, scouts reported they had located Patton's headquarters hidden in a valley over the next ridge. Lt. Hamilton had the entire

Company lay by most of the afternoon and just watch the comings and goings at Gen. Patton's headquarters.

That night it seemed to Grasman he had just gotten to sleep when a toe on his shoulder woke him. It was Lt. Hamilton.

"Go get the squad that engaged the enemy yesterday. I'm giving them the honor of accompanying me to capture the General."

Grasman rubbed the sleep from his eyes. "Sir," he said, "I don't recommend that squad. They have an injured man and besides.."

The lieutenant finished the sentence for him, "'and besides Lewis is the man who shot my horse.' Come on, Sarge, get over it, those men deserve the honor for being the only squad to engage the enemy."

Grasman woke Pvt. Lewis and told him to assemble the squad. He appointed himself squad leader in place of Sgt. Draper in order to be in on the kill. He told himself this would be a new beginning, that Lewis might still be a man to make.

Lt. Hamilton, with Grasman's machine gun squad accompanying him, entered Patton's headquarters and quietly "killed" sentry after sentry until they approached Patton's sleeping quarters.

At 0200 hours, Lt. Hamilton awakened Gen. Patton and told him to get his pants on as he was about to take a horse ride South.

"Call the guard," Patton hollered.

"Sorry, sir," Lt. Hamilton replied, "they've been captured."

He led the general out and put him on a horse. Patton complained about the smell of the animal and wondered aloud how they had gotten so close without his men smelling the horses.

Lt. Hamilton laughed, "Probably overpowered by the smell of the gas fumes, Sir. We just followed the noise those machines make. And by the way, there are four of your tanks buried in the mud less than five miles from your camp. They've spent all their time trying to move while we walked by them. Over the noise of the engines they never heard two hundred men and horses pass within a thousand yards of them."

Grasman turned to his adopted squad. "Nice work, men," he said. Farley looked past him to where George and Jones sat astride their horses and the look Grasman saw on his face made him angry all over again. How dare he smirk at me like that, he thought. He didn't look at George, for at that moment he couldn't endure seeing the mirror of Farley's smirk on that face. He reigned Brute around hard, used his crop on the horse's flank, and rode off after Hamilton and Gen. Patton, leaving the squad to follow him or not.

He didn't hear George say, "Thanks, Sarge."

FT. BLISS - EIGHT

Despite the outcome of the Louisiana Maneuvers, three weeks later orders came down from the Pentagon to Ft. Bliss that the cavalry was to be de-horsed.

Grasman, visiting Draper in sick bay, told him, "We never had a chance of keeping the horses, Jimmy, it had already been decided long ago."

"It's probably for the best," Draper replied, his voice weak and raspy. "It's a new kind of war now. The horses are obsolete. They told me this morning I'm obsolete too."

He lay back on the pillow, exhausted from the few words he'd spoken. Harry knew what they'd found: lung cancer. Draper was one of the few real friends Harry Grasman had and he was going to miss him a great deal. But he couldn't say that and couldn't think of anything more to say.

"It's OK, fella," he stood, his hat rotating in his hands, "you get some rest. I'll see you in a couple of days."

Draper died before Grasman could get back to see him. The guilt of that hung on his shoulders at the funeral. He hovered around Mrs. Draper trying to replace Jimmy for her in some small way. She'd be gone by the end of the week, back to wherever home was and somebody else would move into the house next door. It didn't matter, he'd be busy retraining his men to work with trucks and jeeps instead of horses. Not only was Draper gone, and Dolly gone, but they would all be gone soon.

In less than a week they began taking the horses away. George went out to the stables late one night to say goodbye to Irish.

"They're making a big mistake here," he said as he brushed the big red horse's coat. He combed his tail and braided it, coated his hooves with pine tar and fed him some carrots the cook had given him.

"You look good enough to lead a parade for the brass," George told him and then his voice choked up and he was glad he was alone as a sob escaped from his lips. He leaned his forehead against the Irish's neck and let himself grieve. He knew they were shooting most of the horses. Irish acknowledged his grief by bumping him with his nose. George thought about Grasman and for the first time felt like he really knew how Grasman must have felt when Dolly was shot.

"Maybe I don't blame him for trying to get even with me, Irish. But then, as Dad would say after he'd dressed me down for doing something wrong, it's time to get past that and get some work done." For a moment he thought about the mumbled "Nice job, men" when they'd captured Patton. Then why had he turned so quickly and so angrily and ridden away?

George quietly closed the stable door on his way out. Irish reared and kicked at the stable wall. George guessed he knew they'd never see each other again and was protesting in his own way.

Almost immediately the atmosphere of the post changed. The stables were converted into garages, which were called motor pools. The mystery of when the trucks and jeeps would begin to arrive was solved when the duty roster for the week was posted. Grasman had to provide a dozen drivers to go to Ft. Sam Houston to pick up the trucks. It must have looked like a tiresome and disagreeable detail, because the names George Lewis and Jack Farley headed the list.

"Gonna be one long hot ride," Farley said.

George agreed, thinking about the hard uncomfortable seats in the transport bus. "One thing, though," he said, "no Grasman around to listen to."

They reported to Lt. Giesland right after morning chow. There were 48 "volunteers". Even at that early time of the day it was hot, the inside of the bus stifling. All the windows were pulled open to let in the dust. George saw Grasman standing in the background watching, a pleased smirk on his ugly face.

The bus left post, drove about a mile and stopped at the Southern Pacific railway station. Lt. Giesland made a speech.

"Men, we'll be riding a civilian train to Ft. Sam Houston. You'll be at liberty to move around the train. Meals will be served in dining car A. There will be civilians on this train and I expect everyone to behave. When we arrive in San Antonio we will move as a group to the transport bus and be bivouacked at Ft. Sam for the night. It's a 600 mile drive back, so you'd better get some shut eye when we get there. We'll pull out at 0700 the following morning."

Farley slapped George on the back, a grin splitting his face from ear to ear. "Did you bring the cribbage board, Jiggs?"

Of course he had. It was standard gear in his pack. They boarded the train and had nothing to do but play cards and drink java for twelve hours while the scenery rolled by.

"Farley," Jiggs said after he'd lost three games in a row. "You gotta figure. If they got 200 trucks at Ft. Sam for us less than a month after the Louisiana maneuvers, they've got to have had this planned for a long time."

"You're right," Farley said. "The exercise with the horses against the tanks was supposed to prove to us how superior the machines were. Trouble is, it only proved they made the wrong decision. No wonder Patton was so mad." He shuffled the cards. "You wanna play another hand?"

"Nah," George said, getting up. "Let's go for a walk."

In the car between their car and the dining car, Farley spotted two women alone. "Must be something wrong with them," George said. "With two hundred cavalry men on board why are they still alone?"

Farley looked them over surreptitiously. "They're too old for most of these guys," Farley said. "You gotta remember most of these guys are just outta high school. One of 'ems wearing a wedding band."

George looked now too. Farley was right, the women were in their thirties.

"Let's pick up four cold drinks and stop and visit them on the way back," he said. "Even married women can be charming company when you've been away from females for so long."

When the troops got into Ft. Sam, they found a tent city set up for them. The men didn't have to do anything but sit back and be treated like kings.

George took a shower and sat talking with some of the other drivers. The canteen was open until nine, serving beer and soft drinks. Midnight snacks were available, no charge. When taps sounded at 2200 hours, everybody rolled in.

"Grasman is not going to like this," was the last thing George heard Farley say before he fell asleep.

After breakfast the men lined up to sign for their trucks. Farley wanted to drive one of the big GMC supply trucks. George preferred to drive a jeep or a command car, not that they were given choices, of course. At least Farley got what he wanted.

Each man was issued a thermos bottle full of coffee and a couple of K-Rations before they set out. George threw the K-bricks on the seat of his GMC in disgust and pulled himself in. He wished he had picked up another Snickers bar from the canteen. He hated Spam.

The series Farley and George were traveling in was fifty vehicles long. A series preceded them and two followed; 200 trucks in all. They cruised along at a top speed of 35 mph. They had been told the ride back would take three days.

George hadn't paid much attention to the landscape on the train ride, but now he noticed that the land was greener here. There were passable trees, although they were smaller than back home. Eventually they began to thin into bushes. He saw cattle grazing on the sparse grasses, usually gathered around an oasis of water pumped to the surface by a windmill. Way off to the south he could see the black slope of mountains, but the land he was driving through was flatter than a pancake. For a while, the scenery held his interest, but then it became desert again with mile after mile of endless yucca and mesquite and he began to think Grasman had it planned right this time. Besides the ungodly heat, it was lonely in the truck. The vehicles didn't have windows to roll down but canvas curtains, which rolled up. He resorted to singing to keep himself alert.

They'd been on the road about two hours when the convoy stopped for a break. They got out, stretched their legs, drained the coffee out of their systems and climbed back in. George told Farley it reminded him of his days in the ticks, when he drove truck every day.

Back in the truck, George began to reminisce about those peaceful days in the CCC's. President Roosevelt's depression youth program had rescued George from his life on the road and filled his empty belly in those lean years. It had also allowed him to contribute to the care of the family, which was the most important thing in his young life. The CCC camps were run by the military, but the boys worked for the Conservation Corp. The men in Camp Cooks had built fire roads and planted trees over the lumber-harvested and fire devastated lands. Jones had talked about building bridges in Wyoming.

In 1938, he remembered, there had been a whopper of a snow storm in Upper Michigan. For years people referred to the storm of '38. Before it was over the drifts were so deep the tops of the power lines could be reached without a ladder. The logic in the CCC's wasn't any better than that in the army, and mid-way through the blizzard, George had been sent into town with the Cat snow plow to pick up some supplies. Camp Cooks was about twelve miles from Manistique.

An old couple, Mr. and Mrs. Hall, had a farm about three miles outside town and George usually made a swing through their long driveway to clear it out. In return, Mrs. Hall fed him cookies and sometimes a full home-cooked meal. George could still see the frail old man in his mind's eye. He was tall and thin, with pale freckled skin stretched over his old bones. Mrs. Hall, on the other hand was short and stout with cherry red cheeks.

Just before he got to the Hall's driveway, he came upon a large truck stuck smack dab in the middle of the road. A young man, poorly dressed for the storm, was trying to shovel enough snow from in front of the tires to get some traction. George hooked up to the truck and freed it from the drift, but a dozen yards down the road the truck was stuck again.

"I could pull you out again, but it wouldn't do any good," George said. The snow was coming down so fast and blowing so furious now it wasn't safe to be out. "Let's go inside and warm up. Mr. and Mrs. Hall will give us some coffee."

"I can't leave my truck out here," the driver answered. He pointed out what George hadn't noticed, the truck was a beer truck. "The beer will freeze and I can't afford to pay for a load of frozen beer."

"Let's ask Mr. Hall if we can put it in the barn," George said. "We're not going anywhere for a while."

Mr. Hall was at the door before they even knocked. He said the barn wasn't heated, they'd have to bring the cargo into the living room.

Pretty soon the old farm house was filled with cases of Busch beer. George and the beer truck driver had a regular holiday. For two days they had plenty of good home cooking, nice warm beds, and a beer now and then. When they left, Mr. Hall gave George a full length coon-fur coat to supplement his CCC issue army clothing.

The convoy began to slow down as George reminisced. He saw the trucks ahead of him pull into a large parking lot and followed. A mess camp had been set up in the desert just for the convoy drivers.

"Grasman, eat your heart out," Farley yelled to George as he swung down from the big Jimmy he was driving. "Did you dream it would be this cushy?"

Lunch was hot ham and sweet potatoes with fresh bread and chocolate cake for dessert. After an hour of napping in the shade of the big tent, they hit the road again. That evening they found another large tent camp set up to receive them. Once again there was an open canteen until 2100 hours, after which they showered and went to sleep in bunks set up in fan cooled tents set on wooden platforms to keep the snakes and bugs out. George bought half a dozen candy bars at the canteen just in case he'd have to eat the K-Rations tomorrow, but once again they found comfortable accommodations at each stop.

The final day they drove alongside the Rio Grande most of the day. Twice George saw horse mounted Border Patrols. There was one mountain he watched, it's peak lost in the clouds. Instead of being dark like the others it looked white, like the sand dunes along Lake Michigan. It was big with hidden slopes sliding down into unknown canyons, places where outlaws could hide out from the posses. He felt like he'd finally seem Zane Grey's Texas

The third afternoon, the Convoy drove through the post gate, down Pleasanton Road and parked in the motor pool. After checking their vehicles in they were free for the rest of the day. Farley and George wandered over to the enlisted men's Service Club. Word there was that Grasman was miffed because the detail hadn't been what he'd envisioned for his two favorite whipping boys.

The next day, Saturday, George was on KP. The following day, Farley was peeling spuds. It seemed like the new strategy was to keep the two buddies apart.

There was another detail heading for Ft. Sam on Tuesday to bring back the next convoy of trucks. When the list went up on Monday, Lewis and Farley weren't on it. The top shirt had them picking up trash again. Late Monday afternoon, Cpl. DeeDee Whitmore came out to Howze Stadium, which wasn't a stadium at all but the large main drill field where the polo games were played. Whitmore found George wandering with his trash bag and told him Lt. Giesland wanted to see him at the motor pool.

When he arrived, Farley was there too. Giesland invited them into his office and asked them to sit down.

"What's the beef between you guys and the first sergeant?" he asked.

George told him about Dolly, the sergeant's horse. When he came to the part about shooting the horse between the ears, the lieutenant began to laugh.

"It's not really funny, Sir," George said.

"I know," Giesland said, "but it is funny. So that's why he took you off the convoy detail, huh?"

"Yes, Sir," Farley said. "We had too good a time to suit him."

"Well, report to me tomorrow morning, fellas. You are back on the detail. Now and every trip until we get all those trucks over here. Sgt. Grasman didn't take it too well when I told him how it would be. I also told him I wanted you men to rest up between trips, so you're off KP for a month."

George saw Grasman later that afternoon when he passed by the orderly room on his way to the PX to pick up some fresh reading material. He waved, but Grasman didn't respond.

Payday came and went while they were on their third convoy run. DeeDee had let everyone but George and Farley know that a supplemental payroll would be distributed. Then Grasman announced at Saturday morning inspection that Lewis and Farley had better pick up their pay by noon or they'd have to wait until the next supplemental payroll came out.

They went in together to pick up their cash.

"You fellas having a good time driving truck?" Grasman inquired as he handed them their pay envelopes.

"Oh, it's alright," George said. "Getting kinda old now. I'd rather be peeling spuds, myself."

Grasman gave him a sharp look and slammed the cover of the cash box. "Insubordinate bastard," he muttered under his breath. "I can see to that for you, private, as soon as the lieutenant releases you from this cushy detail."

"Looking forward," Farley said over his shoulder as they walked out.

FT. BLISS - NINE

Even the barracks had a different look and feel to it after the outfit was de-horsed. And a different smell. The spicy odor of the horses had been replaced by the heavy smell of oil. Cpl. Carl Offenbacher from New York had replaced Sgt. Draper as the rifle squad leader. He was a college kid who had flunked out, not from lack of brains, but from lack of studying. Cpl. Offenbacher liked to have a good time, and he fit in well with the squad.

There were a dozen or so other new faces. One of the newcomers was a tough Italian from Chicago named Sal. He swaggered around like he was the son of a gang boss or something. He was about 23, short with big bulging muscles. Jones warned George that he was a bully.

Sure enough their first meeting came on as a challenge. Sal swaggered in just as George was closing up his footlocker.

"Hey, Jiggs," Sal hailed him, using the nickname his friends called him. "Ya back for good this time?"

"Maybe," was the reply. "You're new here aren't you?" He wanted to add, "don't call me Jiggs," but decided to let it slide for now.

"Been around a while. Name's Pancheri, Sal Pancheri."

"And mine is George, George Lewis." He emphasized George, making it clear he was not to be called Jiggs.

"Where's your bunkmate?" Pancheri asked.

"Liska? Don't know, haven't seen him since this morning."

"Well," Pancheri said, leaning against the bunk while he lit a cigarette. "You see 'em, remind him he owes me ten bucks."

George shook in head in disbelief. "Brad Liska owes you ten dollars?"

That didn't sound like Brad. He was quiet, always reading books and catching butterflies to add to his collection. He seldom went to the service club with the rest of them but when he did he stuck close to George.

"Surprised, huh?" the tough said, his self satisfaction with the shock value of what he had said showing on his face. "Brad's a sissy. Even the name is feminine. And that butterfly collection."

He rubbed his nails on the breast of his shirt and blew on them, a gesture meant to signify a fairy. "But I'm working on making a man outta him."

George didn't answer right away. Brad was an only child who'd been raised in New York City by a widowed mother. He was scared and lonely, feelings Pancheri obviously didn't acknowledge as manly. George dropped the butt of his cigarette on the floor and ground it out. He looked Pancheri right in the eye. Brad was a "sissy" name?

"The way I see it, Sally, it takes one to make one. And, General Bradley might take offense at your view that Brad is a "sissy name" and Sal isn't."

Sal recognized the insult; his face colored and George saw his fists clench, but he didn't otherwise respond.

"I beat him at poker and he hasn't paid up yet," he finally said. "You don't shirk your gambling debts where I come from." He reached up and yanked the blanket from Brad's bunk and threw it back in a crumbled ball.

"Hey," George challenged him, "What'd you do that for?"

"A calling card, Jiggs. Just tell him I'm waiting." With that he turned and left the room.

Jones had been watching from the other end of the barracks. He came over and helped George restore Brad's bunk.

"What was that all about?" George asked.

"I told you the guy's a bully. He forced Brad to play poker with them and won his whole pay check plus ten dollars. He broke up one of Brad's butterfly frames. He picks on him all the time."

"Which bunk is his?"

"There", Jones pointed. It was two bunks down, an upper.

"Let's leave him a calling card," George said.

They heard the cussing late that night when Sal tried to get into his short sheeted bed. The lights were already out so he couldn't see the satisfied look on most of faces in the room as the sergeant yelled an order to pipe down.

In the morning, George sat next to Brad at breakfast.

"You've got to stay away from Sal, Brad," George told him. "Hang with Jones while I'm gone. This Sal is nothing but trouble."

When the men returned to the barracks after breakfast, George's foot locker had been broken into and all his cash was gone.

"Pancheri got it," Jones said.

"I'd bet on it too," George said, "but of course we can't prove it."

"I bet I could beat it out of him," Farley said.

"No, don't do anything," George said. "We'll find a better way to get him."

"Not gonna short-sheet his bed again, are you?" Farley asked in a teasing voice. "That'll teach him good."

"This has gone beyond pranks," Jones put in. "We need to do something to teach him a lesson good."

"Let's wait and see what develops," George said. "Something will come up that we can use to bring him down a peg."

Jones and Farley conceded. They knew the way George's mind worked. He preferred the subtle but definite settlement of differences rather than confrontation and violence. The guys took up a collection, a dime here, a quarter there, and got enough together so George had money for smokes and necessities until next pay day. When Capt. Kelly heard about it the scuttlebutt was he chewed Grasman out for making the distribution of the pay public knowledge. Jones said Kelly even threw a dollar into the collection himself.

The scuttlebutt at the club that night was that the outfit would be shipping out by the first of July. A lot of the men were being given seven-day passes to go home. George and Farley missed out on one because they'd been on the convoy detail. They wouldn't have gone back to Michigan anyway, it was too long a trip, and without Patsy, George saw no reason to go.

The fourth and final convoy detail returned to camp on 26 June. Cpl. Offenbacher told them they had one week before they shipped out.

"Holy cow," George said. "Where are we going?" He was excited about it. He'd been at Ft. Bliss for one year. They'd spent all that time training with the horses and then they took them away. Now, with no real infantry training at all, they were being shipped overseas. But, George reflected, that's the way the army operated.

"Rumor says we're going to the South Pacific, but we might end up in France, for all I know."

George and Farley spent the next week driving trucks loaded with gear down to the railroad where they were loaded on flatbeds. On the morning of 2 July, the Division marched to the train station and boarded. They were heading for Camp Stoneman, California.

AT SEA
July 4, 1943 - July 25, 1943

On the 4th of July, A flotilla of seven ships, five trooper carriers, and two escort destroyers, sailed under the Golden Gate Bridge headed for Australia. The S.S. George Washington carried the 12th Cavalry. It was crowded on board and the troops spent their free time playing cards or just plain lounging.

The Navy furnished mess, but requested extra help from the army on a regular basis. Each time Grasman received a request for galley duty, George and Farley were appointed.

Cookie, a huge Pole from Idaho, was one of the cooks in the officer's mess. George and Farley had been there a couple of times before they started to swap stories, mainly about the depression days and how each had survived.

"Seems like I never had enough to eat," George said. "That's why I don't mind KP duty at all."

"You come, twenty-one bells tomorrow night," Cookie said. "Come down passage C and knock on the door there. I fix you up good."

The next evening Farley and George knocked on the door as instructed and Cookie let them into a galley fragrant with the aroma of baking bread. He gave them a freshly baked loaf.

"You come by every third night and I'd be letting you have one of dese," he said. "But you keep it quiet or the gravy train stops and my ass is in a sling."

They thanked him, and silently thanked Grasman, for the grub and took the warm bread back to their bunks. George shared some with Liska, but nobody else knew of their good fortune.

One night as Farley was returning from picking up the bread, he encountered two swabbies carrying a large pan of sliced ham. As they passed him in the narrow passageway, he took two big handfuls of the meat and stuffed them inside his shirt. They yelled at him, but weren't in a position to give chase. That night he and George had ham sandwiches for a midnight snack.

"This is great," George said between mouthfuls, "but why didn't you bring some mustard?"

By the second week at sea, real boredom had set in. The morale officer set up a boxing ring on the fantail and got some competition going. Quite a few of the guys had boxed in the Golden Glove's program and the boxing ring became a popular event both to watch and to participate in.

One of the men who had been added to the Company at the last minute, Charlie Haskell, had been a professional boxer. He helped men with their technique and set up training routines to get them ready for the tournament that would be held the day they crossed the equator.

Jones and Liska wandered by one day to watch. Charlie's firm well balanced muscles glistened with sweat as he jumped rope.

"Why don't you go ask him to teach you?" Jones said to Brad. "You need to learn to defend yourself."

Brad turned red and said, "Wouldn't it be great if we could get Charlie to work Sal over. Kind of get even for him taking George's money?"

When Charlie paused for a drink of water, Jones spoke to him.

"I've always wondered why you fighters jump rope."

Charlie grinned at them. "Looks like a schoolgirl thing, huh?"

"You said it, not me," Jones answered.

"It's good exercise for stamina and nimbleness on your feet. Fighters have to dance, you know, and this trains you to stay on the balls of your feet." He offered the rope to Brad. "You want to try?"

"No thanks," Brad said. "I wouldn't be any good at it."

"You don't know if you don't try," the big man said. "Anyway, nobody does it good first try. Not on anything."

Jones knew Brad wouldn't box so he steered the conversation in a new direction.

"You met Sally Pancheri?"

"You mean that wop from Chicago, the one who is cocksure he's gonna win the tournament? Yeah, I seen 'im around."

"You think he will win?" Jones asked.

"He's pretty good," Charlie said. "He just might."

"Sure hate to see that," Jones said. "It'll only make him worse to live with. Tell him what he did to you and Jiggs, Brad."

With some prompting from Jones, Brad told how Sal had bullied him and about George' s missing money. "We'd like to even the score, kinda let him know we know he's a thief as well as a bully."

"Not much hope I could train either of you to beat him in the ring," Charlie said, then laughed. "I'm probably the only one aboard who could K.O. him."

"You getting into the tournament?" Brad asked.

"Naw, wouldn't be right," Charlie said. "I'm a pro, I can't box amateurs."

Jones and Liska kept trying to talk Charlie into getting in the ring with Sal and beating the shit out of him. After a day or two, he consented.

"But not the tournament," he said. "That'd be wrong. I'll work on him until he challenges me. Then I'll let you know when to come down and watch."

It wasn't long before Charlie let them know he'd be sparring with Pancheri the next evening. Jones and Liska told the whole Company and by the time the two opponents entered the ring, the area was filled with spectators. Jones and Liska were there along with George and Farley.

Both men were wearing army shorts. They fought barefooted and bare-fisted. Sal's well-muscled chest was covered with tight black curly hair. Charlie was blond and his chest hairless. Charlie was taller than Sal, and could outreach him.

"Sally's a fool to get in there with Charlie," George told his companions.

"He thinks he's super fighter," Jones said. "Charlie egged him on 'til Sal challenged. Charlie's been beaten by some big names and bragged about it. One of them came up from the Glove's program in Chicago and Sal had beaten him once in a training match."

The fighters danced back and forth for a while. Sal threw the first punch and Charlie evaded it. They exchanged jabs but neither made contact with the other. Sal had a good left jab but dropped his guard too soon and landed on his heels.

"Charlie's playing with him," Jones said to no one in particular. "He could've gotten him with a right-left combination just then,"

"Hit him," Brad yelled.

When the second round ended with nothing more than sparring, the crowd began to yell for blood.

"I think Sally's getting tired," George said. "He's moving around flat footed."

Charlie came into the third round grinning. Sal managed to land a light punch on Charlie's chin and then danced away. The next time Sal moved in, Charlie reached out, clamped one of his huge hands on either side of Sal's head and picked him right up off the canvas. Sal tried to throw a punch, but Charlie held him up like a puppet, letting his feet dangle in the air. He turned and looked at Jones. "Where's Jiggs?" he shouted.

Surprised, George stood up and called, "Here."

"Say when," Charlie called.

Charlie had turned and was holding Sal so he could see Brad and George standing just beyond the ropes. Sal's gaze met George's and just for a moment George almost weakened, feeling sorry for the chump. It was evident Sal knew what was coming.

"For Liska," George shouted. Charlie lifted Sal as high as his arms could reach and then let go. He hit him with a right cross as he fell. Sal slumped unconscious on the mat.

"Justice is served," declared Jones, "That bully and thief will think twice before he messes with us again."

The day the flotilla crossed the equator the ship erupted into chaos. There were only two kinds of people on board that day: "wetbacks," those who had crossed the equator before, and "polliwogs" the first timers. Tradition dictated polliwogs had to be initiated, even if they wore brass.

When they neared the center line of the earth, all personnel not on duty assembled on the main deck. The wetbacks formed a double line along the deck, armed with paddles and each polliwog had to run the line. George and his friends took part enthusiastically. The actual hits were few and just glancing blows. At the end of the line the deck had been smeared with kitchen lard. George went sliding headfirst into a pile of life jackets at the end amid cheers from Farley and the rest who had gone before him. They cheered loudly as the commanding officer, Gen. William Chase, ran the line just like everyone else and slid through the grease. At the end of the line he brushed off the hands that reached out to help him up, letting go of his dignity just like the others in the spirit of fun.

"There's an officer I could stand to be around," George observed to Farley. "Not like the shavetails who walk around with their noses so high in the air they're likely to trip on a coil of rope."

Farley laughed. "I find that the higher they rise, the more human they are."

"I wonder if MacArthur is like that?" George mused. "From what I read in the papers, he's an arrogant SOB."

The Equator-Crossing Boxing Tournament had begun early in the day. Much to everyone's surprise, Sal didn't enter the tournament. After his drubbing by Charlie, Sal had licked his wounds for a few days. Then Charlie had looked him up and had a long talk with him. After that the two became fast friends. Sal became trainer for one Tommy Allen. Now, Tommy was a finalist, up against Charlie's man, Ace Thompson. George and his friends were cheering for Ace. Tommy Allen won.

After the fun wound down, a picnic of ham sandwiches, a ration of beer, and watermelon were served on deck. Where they got the watermelon in the middle of the ocean, no one knew.

It took 21 days to cross. The flotilla was a day out of Australia when Farley and George showed up for their routine galley duty. The cook that day greeted them with a smile and a cheery, "Good afternoon, gentlemen."

"Afternoon, Sir."

"You just go along to the freezer and pull out a couple of the biggest steaks you can find there. We've got a special meal to cook today."

They did as he asked, also getting two large spuds and an onion.

"Now you just set up that table there for our guests," he said, handing them a clean white tablecloth. "Use the officer's china." He even produced a vase of flowers from God knows where, which he set in the center of the table.

George had just finished cleaning the fresh vegetables when the cook asked, "How do you want your steaks cooked?"

Farley and George were completely surprised. "We couldn't help but notice you two have served more than half of the galley time requested on this cruise. Those aren't very good odds for a ship load of soldiers. The staff just wanted to say thank you."

While they were eating, Grasman walked in, empty coffee cup in hand. He stopped short when he saw them sitting there eating steak by candlelight, but without a word continued towards the coffee urn. The mess cook challenged him.

"Hold on, soldier. That coffee is for those who are working," he said, "I'm asking you to leave my galley now." To emphasize his control of the galley he gestured at the door with the large carving knife he held in his hand.

Grasman left in a fury, not even glancing at his two enemies. As the door slammed behind him, the cook shook his head. "What is it between you three? The old bear has have been picking on you from the beginning."

George swallowed the last bite of his steak and pushed back from the table. "He's trying to even a score with me because I accidentally shot his horse during a ride-and-shoot contest back at Ft. Bliss." George told him the whole story, and like everybody who heard it, the cook roared with laughter, slapping his knee in delight.

"That's one of the best stories I've ever heard," he said. "Have you had enough to eat?"

Both nodded yes, but didn't refuse the heaping bowl of strawberry ice cream he set in front of them for desert. When they left, the cook shook hands with them and bid them farewell. "I won't be asking for anymore help," he said. "We'll be in port by morning. May God go with you."

CAMP STRATHPINE- AUSTRALIA
July 25, 1943 - January 1944

Brisbane, Australia. The first setting of foot on foreign soil for Private George Lewis and most of the other soldiers who fought in WWII. Brisbane is on the twenty-eighth parallel, about like Brownsville, Texas, the southern most point of the United States. July in Australia is midwinter, so while it was warm it was tolerable.

The gear was unloaded, the troops were loaded into 18 troop trucks and headed north. George drove one of the troop trucks. Farley drove another just in front of him. They traveled fifteen miles north before they left the main road and drove through a makeshift gate. The sign overhead read "Camp Strathpine." There was nothing else there.

"This reminds me of the CCC's" George said to Liska who was riding alongside him. "We went into the woods and had to build everything."

"I never saw any woods outside of Central Park in New York until I joined up," Brad said. "The woods scared me silly. I thought there'd be bears behind every tree and snakes in every brush pile."

That reminded George of a story. "One spring when we were planting trees," he began, "I got myself between a mother bear and her cub. Worse position you can be in with a bear. Had no weapon but my shovel. If you run, they'll follow and they can run faster than you ever thought of going. I could hear the little fella in the brush pile behind me."

"What'd you do?" Liska asked.

"I shouted. I keep yelling at her as I slowly shifted, one step at a time, moving further and further away from the cub. When she saw I was leaving she settled down on her four legs and ignoring me, walked over to recover her cub."

"I think I would'a died on the spot," Brad said.

"You know," George said, stroking his chin with his hand, "That bear didn't scare me half as much as thinking of facing those Japs."

Camp Strathpine was nothing like Camp Cooks. When they finished building the camp, they started infantry training in earnest. They drilled day in and day out, getting only Sunday off. There were no three-day passes, and no where to go if they got one.

There were Aussies in camp with them. George liked those fellas. They were friendly, easygoing sorts, eager to swap stories and bullshit the afternoon away. Of course, the way they talked tickled everyone. They thought the Yanks talked funny too. George decided early on that if he got the chance, was still alive, he meant, he'd come back to Australia after the war. It seemed to him that there was still opportunity here, opportunity he hadn't found in America.

George woke suddenly. An unfamiliar sound had filtered into his sleep. He strained his ears to catch it again between the raucous chirping of insects and normal camp noises.

There it was again. It seemed to come from Brad Liska's sleeping bag. It was the same sort of sound he remembered coming from his little brother's bed late at night after Mother died. Brad was stifling tears.

George slipped quietly out of his sleeping bag and crept across the aisle. He touched Brad's foot and whispered, "Come outside,"

Outside George offered Brad a cigarette. Brad shook his head no. George lit his and motioned for Brad to follow him away from the barracks where they could talk. The night was warm, the overhead sky was clear. They stood without talking for a moment, both looking at the sky.

"I love the stars down here," George started. "It's so much different from home, isn't it?"

At the word "home", Brad sucked in a quick breath and expelled a stifled sob.

"What's the trouble, Brad" George asked. His voice was kind but firm in needing an answer. "You get a Dear John letter or something?"

In the dim light George saw him shake his head no.

"What then? Sal's not picking on you again, is he?"

Brad shook his head again, sucked up the snot running from his nose and blurted out. "My mama is dying."

George put a gentle hand on the boy's arm and guided him into a walk down the path to the mess tent. He was well acquainted with all the cooks and had no problem getting two cups of coffee for them.

He waited until Brad had taken a couple swallows of the hot coffee before he invited, "Tell me about it."

Brad said he'd had a letter from his Aunt saying his mother was in the hospital and they didn't know what was wrong with her.

"Have you talked to the Chaplain?" George asked. "Maybe he can get you a furlough."

"She's probably not that bad," Brad answered.

"I thought you said she was dying."

Brad lowered his head, refusing to look at George. "Aunt Betsy said not to worry; but she's all I got, you know, and I do worry."

George let him talk and for the first time heard Brad's story. He lived on the 18th floor of an apartment building near Central Park with his mother and two of her sisters. His father had jumped from the fire escape after the stock market crash of 1929 when Brad was six years old. The three women had raised him, coddled him, smothered him. He'd enlisted to get away, to figure out how to be a man, at which he felt he'd failed miserably.

"First thing you got to do is stop imagining more than your Aunt writes," George said. "Second thing, don't cry. It doesn't help, and if Sal hears you, like I did tonight, he'll make your life miserable."

They finished their coffee and walked slowly back to the barracks making small talk about stars and butterflies on the way. When they neared the barracks, Brad stopped and looked at George. "Thanks, Jiggs," he said. "You're the best friend a guy ever had."

George balled his fist and touched Brad lightly on the cheek. "Go to bed, fella," he said. "I'll be in in a minute."

Twice a week a courier plane, a C54, dubbed the "milk run," came in carrying supplies from the States. Among the cargo they brought were newspapers. Soldiers lined up to go inside the plane and read the papers. Each person was limited to fifteen minutes and the line formed early to get in. At first George tried to get at the head of the line, but after watching for a while he saw that if he waited until late afternoon and got at the end of the line he could stay long enough to read the whole paper. When the plane left, the Chaplain got the newspapers, which eventually ended up in the library after the censors had clipped them to pieces.

Besides the newspapers and supplies, the flight crew ran a profitable black market in whiskey and girlie magazines. The following week George hung around after reading the papers until the crew was done transacting business and then he approached the pilot.

"You ever take human cargo?" George asked.

"For enough money we'll take anything," he answered.

"How much?" The pilot named his price and George set to work raising it. Jones was good at poker. George and Farley staked him with a month's pay each and he threw in some of his own money. All he had to do was double his stake and they'd have enough to send Brad home on the milk run. The next thing was to get Brad a two-week furlough.

Brad worked in the headquarters office. He got the pass on a ruse that his non-existent brother was going to be in Brisbane for a week, and then typed up a set of orders authorizing his trip to the States. He put them in with a bunch of other papers for the CO to sign.

Brad left on the C54 the next day. Two weeks later, Farley went down to meet him at the landing strip and came back empty. "The pilot said he didn't show and they couldn't wait for him."

"Maybe his mother died and he had to stick around for the funeral," Jones said. Whatever, when Grasman counted noses the next morning and Brad wasn't there, he was listed as AWOL. George felt terrible about it. He gave the pilot twenty bucks to ask around for him when he went back.

Two weeks later when the transport landed again Brad was on it. Grasman was all over him immediately. "Missed my connection in St. Louis," Brad explained.

"St. Louis?" Grasman yelled. "There's no St. Louis in Australia."

"Didn't say there was, Sarge. I meant St. Louis, Missouri." Brad explained about the black market traffic on the transports and how his mother was sick and all.

"You've been reported AWOL, and while I don't want to press charges, you'll have to report to the Captain."

Captain Kelly listened to Brad's story. "This is a little more than AWOL, Private. You had a pass to Brisbane, not to the States."

"My orders are here," Brad said, producing the traveling orders Kelly himself had signed.

After examining the papers, Kelly shook his head and delivered his verdict. "Three days on KP for being AWOL," he said, and then added, "Somebody with the guts to carry out such a plan is OK in my book, but don't let it get around. And how is your mother?"

"She's all right, Sir," Brad said. "Had a bout with flu and they thought pneumonia may have set it, but she got better. Thank you for asking."

A large signboard outside the mess tent displayed a map of the South Pacific. To the left was a blackboard headed "Today's War" where the news was posted for all to read. A big battle for New Guinea was being waged and everybody expected to be sent there almost any day.

Strathpine had a beach where the former horse soldiers began to practice amphibious skills; like climbing down rope nets into LCR's, (Landing Craft, Rubber.) The rope nets were one continuous square made up of smaller rope squares, which, when thrown over the side of the ship, created a ladder from one end to the other. The men scrambled down the seven-foot drop and into a nine-man craft bobbing on the water below. They practiced this over and over until they could load a raft, carrying full packs, in less than three minutes. They practiced beach landings and dug countless fox holes. The days were getting longer and hotter.

One morning the troops were ordered into full packs for a march. George's shirt, wet with sweat, clung to him before they had gone far. The heat was worse than El Paso. Almost without warning they entered a forest unlike anything any of them had experienced before. Within yards of entering, the temperature was noticeably cooler and damper. It was like entering a cavernous room with emerald green walls. A ceiling of tree tops high above let in only filtered light. Vines hung from the trees and giant ferns grew from the forest floor. The soldiers, seemingly awed into silence all at the same time, hushed, and a clamor of unfamiliar birdcalls, (George hoped they were only birds), took over.

Beside him Brad whispered, "Can you see the colors, Jiggs? They're spectacular."

George responded, "I don't know, I see what I always see. Tell me what's different."

"For starters," Brad said, "the greens are so green it gives new meaning to the word; like this was what God meant by green and everything I've seen before was just trying to be green. And...WOW! Did you see that?"

"What," George asked, looking where Brad was pointing.

"A bird," Brad said. "Scarlet red."

George had seen the flash of movement, but the color scarlet had no meaning for him. He saw the contrasting brightness of objects but didn't know what names to put to the various shades they came in. He knew only that what others called blue or red were not what he saw.

Brad continued to report in an excited tone what he was seeing. "There, a bird-- shimmering purple with green and yellow on it."

George saw the bird perched on a woody vine looped between two tree limbs. "It's a parrot," he said.

Just then a butterfly landed on a blossom nearby. Brad stopped and stared at it. "I've never even seen a picture of one like that," he whispered. "And me with no butterfly net. I've got to come back here."

George rummaged in his pack and handed Brad his camera. "Here, he said, "take a picture of it."

"But the black and white won't capture the colors," Brad said. "It's a shimmery green or maybe purple, with yellowish veins. It changes color every time it flicks its wings."

They had to keep moving, so the first butterfly was left behind. At the end of the day Brad reported he'd seen at least nine species he'd never even seen pictures of, plus several he recognized. He was in agony over the lost opportunity for collecting and vowed never to leave camp again without a net. Jones found a dead butterfly on the forest floor and offered it to Brad, but Brad shook his head explaining it would crumble to dust without a 'proper death.'

NEW GUINEA
JANUARY 1944

NEW GUINEA - ONE

George had found a comfortable place on the ship to lie back and catch forty winks. In his mind he did a "walk-a-bout" of Camp Strathpine. The Aussie's call any sloping valley a strath. This one had quickly become like home to George and he was sad to be leaving it behind.

Like everyone else he'd written a letter home to his Dad, from "someplace in Australia" saying they were being moved, but didn't say where. The censors would have cut it out anyway. George wondered about the rest of the family. Everyone except his oldest and youngest sisters were in uniform somewhere. It was now January, 1944, and if the papers were right, the enemy was on the run. The job of the Cavalry was to chase them down.

The entire division landed on the coast of New Guinea at Oro Bay, unopposed. It was hot and humid. The place had the sour odor of swamp muck and it hung heavily. Farley said it first. The guys were sitting on the ground during a rare break from jungle training, playing smear and slapping at bugs, sweat dripping from every pore.

"What are we fighting about here?" Farley asked, dropping a jack on George's ten. "It rains every morning and we wallow in mud. Then there's a dust storm every afternoon. I say let the Japs have it."

DeeDee Whitmore had come up behind them and heard this. "You short-sighted assholes," he said, "The Japs want it to build an airbase so they can attack Australia."

"Hell, DeeDee," Farley drawled, "Everybody knows that. Relax and make conversation sometime, why don't ya? It being all about airbases doesn't change the fact that this is the hell-hole of creation."

Whitmore ignored him. "Pvt. Lewis, Sgt. Grasman wants to see you, pronto."

George stood up and put his shirt on. The afternoon dust storm was beginning to blow across the compound. The leather shoes he'd been issued had rotted away within two weeks of landing and he was wearing a pair of sandals woven out of grass. He'd given a fuzzy-wuzzy a pack of smokes for them.

"Grasman don't like your shoes, ask him for some new ones," Jones called after him. "Get some for all of us."

What Grasman probably wanted, thought George, was to harass him about something. The last time he'd tried, it had backfired on him. It was when they were loading on the transport ships at Brisbane. Grasman had had them in formation, at parade rest, waiting for a call from the Navy loading master for their turn to walk up the gang plank. His company had moved up to be next to load and George was the first man in the right-hand file, close to the foot of the gang plank. Farley was quite a ways back and in from George, but they were shouting back and forth to each other.

Farley shouted, "Ask Grasman if I can go to the latrine."

"Ask him yourself," George called back. Grasman was standing right across from George and could hear them, but there were so many conversations going on he might not have been paying attention.

Just then, a young second lieutenant, who was not part of their troop, came by struggling with a heavy valise in addition to his normal gear. He dropped the valise in front of George and pointed at him. "Soldier, carry that bag aboard for me."

The order was illegal; no one, even of a higher rank could command a soldier without first getting permission from the first sergeant. George looked at Grasman who was aware of the lieutenant and his order. He nodded George should comply with the order and help the man get his belongings aboard.

In Grasman's eyes this was an embarrassment for George because it was extra duty, and that suited him just fine.

George replied, "Yes, Sir," to the lieutenant and stepped forward to pick up the black leather valise. No wonder the lieutenant had been walking lopsided with it, the valise was very heavy. George could hardly lift it, but he hefted it up onto the hand rail and slid it along. He knew the entire Company was watching and he also knew from the way the bag felt what was in it. He looked down and saw there was an area of open water between the ship and the dock. The upward slope was steep and just as he reached the point where the water was below him, he let the bag slip. It fell over the side and hit the edge of the dock. The impact broke the valise open and the dozen or so bottles of whiskey that were inside crashed and broke.

The entire Company broke into hand clapping and cheers. Grasman and the other sergeants blew their whistles trying to call everyone to order. Grasman's scar stood out white against his face as it always did when he was angry. George turned to look up the gang plank, but the lieutenant had vanished. George strolled back down the gang plank and took his place in formation. Once order was restored, Grasman relaxed the men to parade rest again.

"He's gonna get you now," Jones said.

"Not a thing he can do," George told him. "Grasman issued an illegal order to me, which I carried out, and the lieutenant was carrying whiskey aboard a ship, which is strictly forbidden."

"Did you know what was in the valise?"

"I guessed it from the way it sat on the railing," George said. "If I'd tried to carry it aboard, I got to thinking what would happen to me when the Navy purser stopped me at the head of the gang plank. It would've been my ass in a sling, not the shavetail's. At least that was what Grasman was hoping. So, I just waited until I was up high enough for everything to break on impact and I pushed it over."

"You think he set you up?"

George nodded. He had been sure of it.

That's why he couldn't help wondering what Grasman could possibly want now. Was he going to be sent on some suicide mission? He'd been expecting Grasman to do so. Patrols moved out every day, but they never saw any Japs. The troops who had fought over the Owen-Stanleys had some terrible tales to tell and the reality of what they were doing had finally hit them. For several days now, George had been aware of some apprehension gathered low in his gut. It stayed there, always ready to jump if he let himself out of the current moment.

George took his time walking up the line of tents to the command camp. Grasman was sitting on a log, whittling, chatting with a young lieutenant. The louie had his back to George and he hung back until Grasman acknowledged him.

"Lewis," Grasman stood and dusted the wood shavings from his lap. "This fellow says he knows you."

The lieutenant turned. George said, "Holy Socks" without thinking. It was his brother, Ned. They embraced each other and then both began talking at the same time.

"When I heard the First Cav was here I had to see if you were with them," Ned said.

George couldn't believe his brother was a shavetail. "How'd you make louie?" He asked, " and guess who else is here?" Without waiting for a guess, he told him. "Jack Farley, you remember him."

"Pembine, the fella you worked with at the filling station," Ned said. "Course I do."

"Let's walk in that direction while you fill me in on this shavetail business."

Ned glossed it over, said he'd been recommended after Tarawa and had gone to school in Brisbane for three months. He was one of those 90-day wonders they were turning out to fill the officer gaps. George told him about the louie whose liquor he'd dropped off the loading ramp.

Ned laughed, "You haven't changed a bit, George. Always rebelling against authority. I remember how you got even with Jack Parker for flunking you in algebra."

Then Ned noticed the shoes. "Surely those aren't regulation?"

George told him most of the guys in the outfit had rotted out shoes. Ned sat down and took off his own combat boots. "Trade me your sandals," he said. "I can get new boots for myself."

They traded. The shoes were a perfect fit, better than the issue he'd had before. "What else do you need?" Ned asked.

They reached the men Jiggs had left playing cards and after introductions and a reunion between Ned and Farley, Ned joined the card game. He had fresh money and was almost cleaned out before he stood to take his leave. The next day he came back with another pair of boots for George and three pair of socks. "Consider these a late Christmas present from Uncle Sam," he said. George appreciated the boots, but he meant to trade a pack of smokes the next day for another pair of sandals. He saved the boots for patrol work. He didn't see Ned again, and guessed his outfit must have moved on.

George and Farley walked through the line of tents. It was early evening but that hadn't cooled anything off. The bugs were everywhere; mosquitoes buzzing around constantly. The army issued Atabrine tablets to the men to keep them from getting malaria but the rumors were that they made you impotent. That didn't bother George as much as the awful taste they left in your mouth and the way they turned your skin yellow.

Liska and Jones joined them. At the edge of camp they found a band of the natives sitting around a fire pit. The natives were short black people with fuzzy hair that stuck out every which way from their heads. That's why the soldiers called them fuzzy-wuzzies. Most of the women and kids wore thigh length skirts made of shredded tree bark, which hung from their hips. All of them, even the women, went naked from the waist up. Liska, who never went anywhere without his camera now in case he saw a butterfly, began snapping pictures. At first the naked breasts of the women had been something to stare at, but now it was everyday. The women sat weaving baskets or pounding taro root.

Most of the men spoke a pidgin type of English, enough to communicate on a limited basis. The words were easy enough to understand, but they talked so fast, running sentences together, that it was difficult to get the sense of what they were saying. George made his trade of a pack of smokes for new sandals and sat down beside the native to watch him make them.

This group had been carriers for the Aussies and they wanted to tell about it. "You give three goodfeller cheers all boys look out strong feller master, carry much, you savvy?" They were known as Fuzzy Wuzzy Angels because of their gentleness in carrying the wounded down the steep slopes and through the jungle. Some of them wore the khaki shorts and shirts issued to them, but others wore a rag slung between their legs to protect themselves, with the ends tucked into another rag tied around their waists. The only other clothing they wore was a scarf around their necks. All of them went barefoot. The soldiers were forbidden to do so because of hook worm infecting the ground, and the enterprising fuzzy-wuzzies were quick to see this and garnered many packs of smokes in exchange for the grass sandals they could make to size for you while you waited.

The night darkened. George sat listening to the noises of the jungle, comparing them to the noises of the jungle in Australia. New Guinea had 70 kinds of snakes, including the deadly taipan, the death adder, and the ringed coral. The tidal swamps where the natives lived in stilt houses were crocodile infested. Besides the mosquitoes, there were scorpions, sandflies, and mites. And to Brad's delight, some of the most beautiful butterflies in the world. Farley's few words summed it up right; it was the hell-hole of creation.

The outfit was taking part in an amphibious training problem on 26 February, 1944 when orders came to stop and immediately return to Camp Borio where they began to make preparations for movement into their first live combat.

THE ADMIRALTY ISLANDS
FEBRUARY 1944 - MAY 1944

ADMIRALTY ISLANDS – ONE

The Admiralty Island assault, which began on 29 February 1944, was designated "Brewer Operation," and was undertaken by Alamo Force, composed of units assigned to the Sixth Army. The First Cavalry Division was the nucleus of the task force. The Division, commanded by Gen. Innis P. Swift, was composed of two Brigades, each made up of two reinforced regiments. Capt. Grant Kelly, Sgt. Harry Grasman, and Pvt. George Lewis, were in the 12th regiment of the 1st Cavalry, commanded by Brigadier General William C. Chase. The 12th Cav was the newest of the Cavalry Regiments, having been organized in 1901. Their sister Regiment, the 5th, was the oldest, organized in 1855. Among its past commanders were Robert E. Lee and Jeb Stuart.

Capt. Kelly paced back and forth in the small briefing room. The LST rolled in the high seas, and, although Harry Grasman wouldn't have let on if his life had depended on it, it made him nauseous. The cruise from San Francisco to Australia had been bad, but the constant roll of this small troop carrier

had him green at the gills. He glanced sideways at
Lt. Krantz. It was easy to see that Krantz was
nervous. He was young and had never been in
combat before. Harry felt he had the edge on him
there, although he'd never been in this position
before. In WWI he'd been just one of the soldiers
and they'd never had to make a storm landing. In
the horse soldier days, they'd have been off loaded
on good beaches and transported as close to the
front as possible in trains.

"MacArthur has called the Admiralty Islands
the 'cork in the bottle'," Kelly said. "They control the
entrance to the Bismarck Sea; sentinels at the
Northern entrance." The captain referred to a large
wall map. "See? They block the Japs access to
Rabaul. You already know that we're bypassing a
direct assault on the big Jap bases there and,
instead, are island hopping around it to cut off
supply lines."

The largest island of the group, Manus, was
separated from tiny Los Negros by a shallow, creek-
like strait. The horseshoe curve of Los Negros at the
western tip of Manus formed Seeadler Harbor, six
miles wide and 20 miles long with depths up to 120
feet. On the eastern coast of Los Negros, a smaller
harbor, Hayne Harbor, protected the Momote
airfield, which the Japanese had begun building the
year previous,

"The fifth Cav landed here," Kelly tapped the
beach of Hayne Harbor near the Momote airfield,
"11 days ago, and was met with some resistance,
but the Momote airfield area has now been secured.
The Seventh Cav joined them on 3 March. In the
morning, we're going ashore the same place the
Fifth Cav did, here, at Hayne Harbor. Since that
area is held by our forces, it will not be a storm

landing. Sergeant, have your men ready to start off-loading at 0700."

Grasman felt a letdown over this news. The thought of a landing under fire had had the adrenaline pumping and he had entertained visions of a landing craft holding Pvt. George Lewis being swamped by high waves and then the survivors being gunned down by enemy snipers on the beach. His spirits were revived by the next words of the captain.

"Once on shore assemble our Company in preparation for an assault north to gain control of the Salami Coconut Plantation. Col. Stadler will be in command. The 7th Cav will lead out, and we will follow."

At 0820, after the Navy had fed the men a hot breakfast, the 12th Cavalry with additional artillery, signal, and engineer troops as well as medical detachments, began to disembark from four LST's (Landing Ship, Tank) at Hayne Harbor.

Company C was a rifle Company. It was made up of four Platoons plus a weapons Platoon of two light machine guns and three 60 mm mortars. Each Platoon was composed of four squads of 12 men each. Sergeant Grasman had 240 men to kept track of.

The men waded ashore, their rifles held in firing position. They wore helmets, long-sleeved shirts, and 50 pound packs on their backs. The water in the bay moved in low rolling swells and after an initial threat of being upended, George found his balance and moved with the Platoon toward shore. Thank God, he thought, they didn't have to do this under enemy fire.

By noon everything was in readiness. They advanced across a skidway that had been built by the natives over the narrow strip of sea that split Los Negros just north of the airstrip. The engineer platoons moved out first, clearing the road of felled trees and booby traps. All advance halted several times while the dozers rebuilt road around bomb craters.

"Hurry up and wait," Jones complained. He was sitting on his fully loaded pack, his shirt unbuttoned to catch the occasional breeze.

George grinned across his head at Farley. "Why should it be any different in paradise than it was at Bliss?"

"Hell, this sure isn't my idea of an island in the South Seas." Jones said. "I thought there was supposed to be hula girls in grass skirts and hammocks strung between coconut palms."

"With cool drinks in tall thin glasses," Farley supplied.

"The coconut palms are here," George said, sweeping his arm at the rows of trees that stood between the beach and the airfield where they now waited. The trees were indeed there although the tops of some had been snapped off by artillery fire during the softening up phase of the invasion. Trunks of fallen trees lay everywhere. The beach was 150 yards beyond the rows of coconut palms.

"Yeah, sure," Jones said. "The pictures never show you the damn kunai grass, do they? Or the tangled vines along the ground that trip you up every other step."

Finally they began to move again. The engineers had finished filling a vehicle trap after one of the big trucks had fallen in. It was a ditch about four feet deep camouflaged by canvas stretched flush with the road on a framework of poles and covered with light coral sand. Once the ditch was filled, troops continued to move until they reached the front where the 5th and 7th Cavalries were bogged down. The narrow trail was ankle deep in mud and blocked by mired vehicles.

"Same thing we saw in the Louisiana maneuvers," George muttered to Jones. "The horses would've been through this already."

They sat and waited and waited and waited until word came that the 12th Cavalry was to bypass the quagmire to the west and continue the advance.

The troops moved forward in combat formation, weapons at port arms, each man covering another. Three amphibian tanks, known as buffaloes, accompanied the foot soldiers, but the three light tanks they'd come ashore with were mired down back with the 7th Cav. Twice they heard short bursts of gunfire from the forward troops, but the enemy inside the pillboxes withdrew on contact. The way was littered with abandoned Japanese equipment, remnants of their hasty retreat.

They approached the coconut plantation that was their objective very cautiously. It looked pretty much like the one at Hayne Harbor.

"I thought the trees would have sticks of salami hanging from them," Brad joked. "Didn't they say we were heading for the Salami Plantation?"

Before anybody could reply, a barrage of enemy fire caused them to hit the ground. The numerous buildings at the center of the plantation were apparently where the retreating Japs had gone. Cpl. Offenbacher crawled forward. George and the rest of his rifle squad followed. The buffaloes were in front of the troops, firing canister bombs into the buildings. A burst of machine-gun fire came from their left, seemingly from a well-camouflaged bunker. "Use your grenades," Offenbacher called.

Under their first live fire, Brad froze. George grabbed his foot and pulled him down. "You gotta shoot, Brad. Get them before they get you." The squad began laying down a shower of firepower to cover Jones who stood and lobbed the first grenade into the bunker. The exchange continued for what seemed like eternity, each solider in turn lobbing a grenade into the bunker. Brad stood to throw and then began to run toward the bunker.

"Where the hell are you going?" Offenbacher screamed at the crazed soldier. "Get down." The enemy in the bunker opened up and the force of the bullets spun Brad around. He hit the ground facing his friends.

George started to crawl forward to bring him back. "He's dead, Lewis," Offenbacher screamed. "Leave him."

But Brad wasn't dead. He rolled his head and looked straight at George. His face was covered with blood. "I'm going after him," George said. "Cover me."

The riflemen laid down a covering fire while George crawled forward to where Brad lay. He was bleeding everywhere and George couldn't tell where the worst wounds were. He grabbed Brad by the back of his shirt collar and began crawling back, pulling his friend behind him.

Safe behind a small mound, George held Brad in his arms. How many times had Brad told him how scared he was? Damn, it wasn't fair to send a kid like this into hell and expect anything of him. He hollered as loud as he could, "Medic!" He yelled it again and again, but nobody came. He felt Brad grip his hand harder and he bent down and kissed the bloodied cheek of the young man. The grip released suddenly and George knew Brad was dead. He lowered him gently to the ground, wiped his bloodied lips on his sleeve and then emptied his rifle clip into the enemy bunker. By that time, the occupants of the bunker were all dead. The other men in the company had already avenged their fellow's death. First battle, first loss. The entire battle had lasted less than half an hour.

A foothold at Seeadler Harbor had been won. In the harbor area were large amounts of supplies and equipment, gasoline, ammunition, radios, food, and boxes of propaganda pamphlets all hastily abandoned by the Japanese. While the headquarters company investigated these finds, the foot soldiers began to dig foxholes in which to spend the night.

George worked alongside Jones. Neither of them said anything for a long time. "Shooting a man's not like shooting a deer," George said finally.

"Sure ain't," said Jones. "Even if they are Japs,"

"Did he say anything?" Carl asked.

"No," George answered. "He just looked at me. He was afraid right to the end."

ADMIRALTY ISLANDS – TWO

George carried a 30-caliber machine gun, supported by ammo carriers and rifles. His assistant gunner was Jim, from Nebraska. Jerry Cribar carried the ammo. Jones, Franco Depazsolis, and ordinary, Brad, supported the machine gun with rifles and also carried additional ammo. In addition to a rifle, Farley also carried a flame-thrower. The automatic weapons covered the front line positions, so he sat front and center of the tight perimeter they had secured around the Salami Plantation. The rifle squad occupied four fox holes around the automatic weapon, one on each side and two in the rear. Nebraska Jim shared the foxhole beside the machine gun with George. Jones and Franco were in the hole on his left flank; Jerry, minus Brad, on the right. Farley and Carl occupied the other front hole. The password that first night was Liska.

The noises from the jungle made them all jumpy. They'd been told there were no man-threatening things out there except Japs. The unidentifiable sounds kept George alert. Jim was sleeping. The blackness was total. Black as death. *What was death?* George let his mind go with the question. *What could it mean to cease to be? Was*

*there a heaven? Or a hell? Was there a God? If there
was, why didn't He stop this insane war?*

How? What would God do to stop it? War was
started by men and could only be stopped by men.
There was a mini-war between him and Sgt.
Grasman. *And I started it,* George thought.
*Accidentally. No he'd started it by refusing to believe
it was an accident, and I don't know how to stop it.
Will it escalate to killing? Will he shoot me in the back
if he gets the chance? Might be.* He'd heard some
stories of actual murder in the trenches when they
were in Guinea. He'd met a guy whose only job was
to investigate such accidents.

A different noise, a stealthy rustling, came
from his left, camp side. *Grasman?*

"Who goes there?" he called into the dark.
Stupid thing to do, he immediately thought. *If it
was the enemy I've just told him where I am.*

"Liska," came a low angry whisper. "Shush,
for god's sake, there's probably Japs out there just
waiting for a target." It was Franco, his ammo
carrier.

"What are you sneaking around for?"

"Gotta take a leak. Cover me, will ya?"

"For pete's sake, get back in your hole. They
told us to stay put and make the best of it."

Offenbacher whispered. "Get it over with and
get back in that hole. Don't anybody else budge."

The rest of the night passed without further
incident

20 March 1944. Company "C" was advancing
up the Mokerang Peninsula, north of Salami. The
approximately 240 men moved in two single file
columns down either side of a dirt and coral road.
The sun beat down on them and reflected up from

the white coral road. The machine gun crew walked near the end of the column. George carried the machine gun and tripod on his back, and a rifle held ready. Jones and Franco carried their rifles and ammo for the machine gun. Across the narrow road from them walked Farley, carrying a flame-thrower, along with Nebraska Jim and Jerry. Carl was forward with the other squad leaders conferring with Captain Kelly. Low conversation was allowed, but not much was being said.

"Hey, George," Farley said, "look at that." That was a small abandoned Jap truck, tilted at a dangerous angle above a ditch filled with water. "What do'ya think's wrong with it? It doesn't look damaged."

"Probably out of gas," George answered.

"Let's take a look," Farley said.

"Be careful, it might be booby-trapped," Jones warned, but Farley was already taking the top off the gas tank. "Half full," he said. "I'm gonna look under the hood."

George looked at the retreating columns of soldiers. Nobody noticed that they had stopped. The few troops behind them just walked on by.

Farley lifted the hood and began to check wires and hoses. "We're getting left behind," George warned.

"Let 'em go. We'll catch up when I get this baby running. My feet are sore from all this walking."

The jeep looked like a model "T" Ford except there was a gear shift on the floor. It had a four-cylinder engine, and small tires made of steel. Farley tinkered under the hood while Jones sat behind the wheel. Finally it kicked over. Jones moved aside and let Farley drive. George sat in the passenger side with his machine gun; the other three men rode in the small truck box, between its high sides.

By the time they got the truck running, the company had moved out of sight. They hadn't driven more than a mile when the road they were following became three. One track veered left, one right, and one continued. "Which way?" Farley said.

The rocky coral base of the road made it impossible to discern which way their outfit had gone. "Turn right," George said. "They can't be far. If we don't run up on them in ten minutes we can backtrack and take the left fork."

They began to see jungle growth along the chosen road. It became thicker and thicker as they progressed. Moisture dripped from the large leaves overhanging the road and it was cooler. Rounding a curve they were suddenly on a wooden bridge arching over a fast-moving river.

"Holy cow," George said, his eyes keen and always watching ahead. "That's a Jap standing at the other end of the bridge."

"Well, this is a Jap truck," Farley said. " Keep your face hidden."

The guard glanced up at the truck, apparently recognized it, and waved them by. Farley continued to drive through a good sized Jap camp. George, looking out from under his cap, which was pulled low over his face, saw five Jap soldiers cooking rice over an open fire. The road took a turn and the men found themselves out of sight of the camp.

"What are we going to do?" Jones asked. He was looking at George for an answer.

"We turn around and drive right back out," George said. "If we're spotted, toss grenades and shoot like the dickens. Farley, you'll have to drive like hell and get us across the bridge. Franco, you take the flame-thrower, and if we're spotted you set the bridge on fire behind us. If we're not spotted, just keep low 'til we get the hell out."

It must have been because of the Jap truck and because the men in the camp were all occupied with fixing their supper's, but no one paid any attention as the truck came back though the middle of the camp and was again waved through by the single guard at the end of the bridge.

Across the bridge and out of sight, Farley gunned the engine. Just as they were re-approaching the split in the road, the right front wheel fell off and went rolling down the road in front of them. The truck skidded for fifty feet and came to a stop.

"Whew," Franco said as he climbed out of the box, "that was close." He handed the flame-thrower to Farley. "I don't know how to use this thing," he said.

"Well, we're in bigger trouble now," said George, "here comes our outfit."

"How'd they get behind us?" Farley wanted to know.

The infantry moving up the road was not Company "C" but Company "F". The men waved their arms in the air, hoping the column would recognize them as Americans and not start shooting at them because they were with the Jap truck.

Capt. Melling was at the head of the column. He stopped and inquired what the men wanted. George told him what had happened and about the Jap camp on the right fork of the road.

"You fella's pulled a really stupid stunt," the captain said, "but the information you have is extremely valuable to us. Are Kelly and Grasman aware you left the column?"

"No, Sir," George said.

"You take this note to Capt. Kelly," Melling said, scribbling something on a note pad. "Your Company was to take the left fork and we were to turn right. We'll go straight now. Double time it and catch Kelly before he goes too far from the objective."

The columns were at rest not too far up the left fork. Grasman had discovered they were missing. When he spotted the six men coming up the road, he ran towards them, waving his arms and cursing loudly.

"I've got you now, Lewis," he shouted, shaking his fist in George's face. "You didn't have permission to leave the column. I'll have you shot for desertion. You won't get away with your insubordination this time."

"I have a message for the captain," George told him, waving the piece of paper from Capt. Melling under Grasman's nose.

"I'll take that," Grasman grabbed for the note.

"Sorry, sergeant," George said. "I was told to give it directly to Capt. Kelly and tell him what we found."

"Gentlemen," Capt. Kelly said as he approached. "Keep your voices down, this is supposed to be a quiet approach. What's going on here?"

"This man and his crew deserted the column a couple miles back and were trying to sneak back in without being caught," Grasman said. "I'm charging them with desertion."

"We met up with Capt. Melling and his outfit, Sir," George said to the captain. "He gave me a message for you."

Kelly read the message and invited George to walk with him. "Bring the rest of his men forward," he told the astonished first sergeant.

"It was Farley's skill with motors got the truck going," George said as he explained to Kelly what they had done and what they had seen. "Melling said to tell you he's going straight instead of right, which would have put him right into the Jap camp."

"Taking that bridge is our objective," the captain said. "Our maps are wrong, we thought it was on the road that went straight. We thought that by covering his right and left flank we could pinch the enemy out. I don't condone what you did, but the information you got has undoubtedly saved a lot of lives."

"That doesn't mean you'll get away with it," Grasman put in. "You'll be punished."

"Nothing of the kind, sergeant," Kelly said. "They left ranks and acted stupidly, but I will not hear of punishment. The matter is ended here. Is that understood?"

"You men are dismissed," the Captain said. "Thanks again, and from now on, keep your noses clean."

"Yes, Sir," they said in unison.

Evening had come down suddenly on the camp. Capt. Kelly and his squad leaders were gathered around the radios. Captains Kelly and Melling coordinated their plans for taking the bridge. When the radios fell silent, Kelly sought out his first sergeant.

"Grasman, those men who brought the information to us. Wasn't that Private Lewis, the one who shot your horse?"

"The same," Grasman growled.

"And the one who was able to get the truck started, who is he?"

"Friend of Lewis, name of Jack Farley. I understand they knew each other as civilians."

"Hell of a team," Kelly remarked.

"They're a couple of insubordinate bastards." Grasman shot back.

"Maybe so," Kelly said, "But they're thinking men, a rare breed nowadays."

"They're also the ones who let that young man fly back to the states when we were at Strathpine." Grasman reminded them.

"Wasn't that the young man who was killed taking Salami?" Kelly asked. "I'm glad he did that, saw his mother before it happened. God, I hate to lose good men. I want Lewis and Farley and the four men who were with them to get some rest tonight. See that they aren't on guard duty."

Grasman moved off into the night grumbling. Guard duty was exactly where the six men were. He sent a detail to relieve them.

Three days later, after a circuitous maneuver, the two companies attacked the Jap encampment by the river from the rear. There were no American casualties. The Jap camp was wiped out and the bridge—a vital link to the tip of the Mokerang Peninsula and the two islands beyond it—was taken.

ADMIRALTY ISLANDS- THREE

The mopping up operations on the Admiralties went on until mid April when the 12th Cav moved to the Salami Plantation and settled down to some richly deserved rest to be followed by more intensive training. The refrigeration, bakery, and laundry companies moved in and set up, making living in the tropics almost pleasant.

Mail from home and personal packs left behind during the landing caught up with George and Farley. After claiming their belongings, the two found a patch of shade next to the mess tent and began to sort things out. George had three letters from home, one from his sister, and two from Dad.

The first letter from Dad filled him in on the whereabouts of the rest of the family. Two of them, Frank & Ned were in the South Pacific. He already knew about Ned, having seen him in New Guinea. One of the pair of shoes Ned had given him were in the duffel bag, which lay at his feet. His sister was in England, a First Lieutenant in the Women's Army Corp or WAC. His other two brothers were fighting in France and China.

The second letter contained a draft notice for one George W. Lewis from the U.S. Navy and a small clipping from the Iron Mountain weekly newspaper.

"What the hell?" George exclaimed turning the yellow paper over and reading it again. "Look at this, Farley. The Navy wants me."

The newspaper clipping was a Navy recruiting notice for men who were color-blind to train as spotters for gunnery crews. Seems the Navy had discovered what George had realized early on. Camouflage actually made enemy positions easier to spot. He didn't see much color, but light bounced off the camouflaged stuff different. He didn't know what regular people saw, but he saw the netting and the multi-colored shields as plain as day.

"What are you gonna do about the draft notice?" Farley asked.

George stood up, "Guess I'll have to show it to Grasman. It doesn't seem right to just ignore it."

George found Sergeant Grasman polishing his boots. "Sergeant?" George used the full title instead of Sarge like most of the men. The formality emphasized the strain between them.

Grasman didn't look up from his task. "What is it Private?"

"My mail had this in it and I need to know what to do with it." He handed Grasman the draft notice and waited while he read both that and the clipping.

"Are you color-blind?" Grasman asked.

"I am."

"Can you see through camouflage like they say?"

"I can."

"Why haven't you said so?"

"The Navy and the Merchant Marines both turned me down because of it. When the Army didn't catch it, I kept quiet. I figured if I let on they'd send me home on a medical."

Grasman had stood up during the conversation and now began to walk toward the Headquarters tent. George hurried to catch up with him.

"Maybe we will," Grasman said, his voice sounding hopeful. "Then the Navy can have you"

They found Capt. Kelly playing cards in front of the officer's club. Grasman waited until the poker hand played out and then interrupted.

"Pvt. Lewis has a problem, Sir," Grasman said. "Looks like we'll be able to send him back to the States."

Grasman explained that Pvt. Lewis was color-blind and not medically fit for the Army.

"But the Navy wants him, Sir. Seems like they can use color-blind men." Grasman handed him the notice and waited while Kelly read it.

"Have you tested him, Sergeant?" Kelly asked.

"No, Sir," Grasman said. "But he told me it's true."

Addressing George for the first time, Capt. Kelly said. "Report back to me in two hours, Lewis. We'll test this theory."

"Yes, Sir." George saluted and left. He walked across the hard coral beach deep in thought. Would he rather leave Farley and the rest of his squad to become regular Navy, or stay here? He'd dreamed of going to sea ever since he'd ridden a Great Lakes iron ore carrier through the locks at Sault St. Marie when he was 12. Before the War he'd tried to join the Merchant Marines. When they turned him down, he joined the CCC's.

"What'd he say?" Farley asked as soon as George joined them. He told them about the upcoming test. "Grasman is pretty sure they'll send me back. Wishful thinking, maybe. Maybe I'll have a choice. What do you guys think?"

"I say get outta here," Farley advised.

"You wouldn't be on the ships," Jones pointed out. "You'd be flying."

"Never been in an airplane," George said. "I think I'd like that."

"Probably by the time they got you trained it'd all be over," Farley said.

"I thought about that," George said. "They trained me for almost two years before I ever got into combat. I'm sick of training, being treated like dung by everybody. For that alone, I'd sooner stay here."

The two hours passed quickly. George reported to Capt. Grant Kelly. A crowd of majors, lieutenants, and platoon leaders stood nearby. Farley and Jones and the rest of his squad hovered in the background, as did Grasman. George was asked to point out the five camouflaged targets which had been prepared. He quickly located all five.

"Well, Lewis," Kelly said, "that was pretty amazing. We'll tell the Navy that you're already on active duty with the 12th Cavalry. Leave the notice with my secretary to handle."

"Sgt. Grasman," he called.

"Sir," Grasman rushed forward and saluted.

"I'm recommending this man be promoted to corporal. Put him in charge of his squad. From now on they are a camouflage spotting unit. Find out if any other men in our Company have this ability."

"Yes, Sir." Grasman said. He had lost his usual snappy manner and walked away with his head slightly down.

"Looks like Ol' Harry is a little disappointed with the way things turned out," Farley observed.

"Are you?" Jones asked.

George stroked his chin. "I don't think so. I'd've missed you guys. Like I said, I wasn't looking forward to months of training again."

"Then let's go find some of that local hooch they make outta coconut juice and celebrate," Farley said. "It ain't beer, but it's wet."

LEYTE ISLAND, PHILIPPINES
October 1944 - January 1945

LEYTE ISLAND - ONE

The Philippines are a group of islands in the South China Sea, 500 miles off the eastern coast of Asia. The archipelago has two large islands. Mindanao, the southernmost island is shaped like a molar tooth with roots. Luzon, the larger northern island, is shaped like the head of an octopus. The capital, Manila, is on Luzon. Between these two big islands are several good sized islands and thousands of small ones. It is 1100-odd miles from northern tip to southern tip, as far as from Detroit, Michigan, to the gulf coast of Alabama.

The Japanese had invaded the Philippines within hours of bombing Pearl Harbor and had spread from there south into the other islands of the South Pacific. Now MacArthur's Sixth Army was close to reversing their expansion. One by one, the allies had driven the Japanese out of the islands and MacArthur's famous promise "I shall return" was close to being realized.

The Island of Leyte is above Mindanao and is partially protected from the ocean winds by Samar, which is larger and borders the Philippine Sea. Leyte Gulf is between the two islands. It is this long mountainous island MacArthur chose for his return to the Phillippines. His invasion force was the battle hardened First Cavalry Division made up of the 7th, 12th, 5th and 8th Regiments.

It was late October, the dry season in Leyte. The Cavalry's arrival on the western shore triggered one of the major naval battles of the war, the Battle of Leyte Gulf. The Japanese had expected the Allied armies to storm the beach further north, at the entrance to Ormac Valley. Instead they came ashore on the southern beaches.

George sat on his bunk aboard the Navy ship and checked his weapon for the eighth time. Despite the recommendation for promotion Capt. Kelly had made, Lewis remained Pvt. Lewis, a point that pleased Sgt. Grasman. His satisfaction may not have been so great had he known that it made no difference whatsoever to George Lewis.

The tension in the tight quarters had an odor; fear intensified the sour smell of perspiration. Reveille had sounded hours earlier and they had dressed under the red blackout lights. The Navy had fed them the last hot meal they were likely to have for several days. The Chaplain had come by an hour ago and prayed with them and left several palm-sized Gideon Bibles. Jones now sat reading from one.

George stood and lit a cigarette. The roar of the big guns from the Navy covering fire made talking impossible even if they'd been inclined to talk. Any conversation was whispered, as if they were in a church. When the order came to assemble on deck, it was almost a relief.

George had hoped seeing the action would be less disturbing than just hearing the constant boom of the guns, but all he could see was a pall of lazily billowing thick smoke that obscured the landing shore. It was raining. So much for the dry season. There were dozens of ships in the sea around them, battle cruisers 'softening' up the beach for the landing, and troop carriers waiting for passengers.

"Rendezvous your landing boats at a line of departure 5000 yards from shore," they were being told over a loud speaker. "The flotilla will advance abreast as close to the beach as possible and then you'll wade ashore."

They'd practiced this over and over for months, both in Strathpine and from the camps on the Admiralty Islands. "The water is shallow," the voice continued, "and the beach is firm coral sand, but it's narrow. Hit the beach and advance inland past the line of coconut trees as quickly as possible."

If you can get that far, George thought. *This is not going to be a picnic like the Admiralty landing.*

The troops went over the side and down the ropes to board the landing craft which bobbed like corks on the rolling sea. Each man carried all his own equipment in a fifty pound pack. George carried a rifle plus part of the light machine gun. Jones carried the other part and the rest of the crew carried the machine gun ammunition.

One of the men close to George and his troop apparently passed out as he went over the rail. A swabbie above reached out with a long gaff hook and pulled him back aboard the ship.

"Why didn't I think of that?" Farley shouted to George.

Rocket and gunboat LCI's, preceded by amphibian tanks, accompanied the invasion flotilla. The rocket ships continued to lay down a heavy barrage of fire which covered the beach and reached inland to a depth of 1800 yards in an attempt to leave the enemy incapable of organized resistance.

It was mid-morning. The landing craft carrying George stopped 100 yards from shore and the 30 men inside slipped over the side to wade ashore. George struggled to get his footing and still keep his rifle dry. A wave of salt water filled his mouth. He cursed and spat. The taste of the salt lingered in his mouth. Beer was the only thing he knew that rinsed the salt taste away quickly. *"Hell of a thing to be thinking of now,"* he muttered to himself.

Company C was in the second wave and the initial light resistance of small arms and machine gun fire from the enemy had been silenced. The heavy boom of the navy guns had also ceased, but the noise was still deafening because of the planes flying overhead. They were American planes, keeping the Japanese planes from strafing the troops coming ashore. The planes were flying low, less than 100 feet above the ground.

The 12th Cav came ashore in between the 5th and 7th regiments. Their objective was Highway 101, which ran parallel to the beach about a mile inland.

George and his squad crossed the narrow strip of sand quickly. The firm coral beach had been pounded into a quagmire of mud by the rain and the troops that had preceded them.

Beyond the muddy beach and the line of coconut trees, George and his men waded into a real swamp that lay between them and Highway 101. Mosquitoes swarmed in small black clouds around them. George wondered if anything more noxious, like crocodiles and water snakes were in the water. Soldiers with guns at the ready stood on both banks of the swamp, maybe they were there to shoot the crocs if one showed up. The thick, smelly, water quickly reached waist high. When the depth increased even more, George swore under his breath and turned around to see how the others were doing.

"Can't get the ammo wet," he called back. "We'll have to make more than one trip." They turned back and rearranged their loads. It took them three trips, holding their packs over their heads as they waded, and often floundered, their way across the swamp.

"Now there's a real leader for you," George said when Gen. Chase, their regimental commander, waded into the swamp and began directing traffic. An hour later, on their third and final ferrying, they watched a second lieutenant in a clean uniform approach Chase on a plank walk laid from grass clump to grass clump for him to walk on. He was protected by an umbrella carried by an accompanying corporal. He offered Chase a plate of hot food.

"What the hell do you think this is soldier, a picnic?" they heard Chase explode at the lieutenant. "Give that food to that man back there," he pointed at a GI who lay on a stretcher a few feet away. "He needs it more than I do". He also dismissed the umbrella and plank laying detail and made the lieutenant wade through the swamp to reach the wounded man's side. When the food had been consumed, Chase called the lieutenant back to him and ordered him to join the people carrying supplies across the swamp.

At about 1800 hours, as they advanced across still marshy, but relative solid ground, they heard gunfire to their left, which lasted around ten minutes. Word passed down that an enemy pillbox had been encountered and squashed. We'd lost one man and had two wounded, they said.

By 1915 hours, the 12th Cavalry had crossed Highway 101 and began to form its night perimeter.

They ate K-Rations for breakfast the next morning while slumping in shallow foxholes. Digging a proper foxhole in coral was impossible. Word spread that Gen. Douglas MacArthur had waded ashore at the same place they had landed with news cameras filming the whole thing, and uttered the words he'd been rehearsing for three years, "I have returned."

"I'd like to have seen that," Jones said.

"Hell, man" George told him. "You saw a real general in action yesterday when Chase waded into the swamp with us and told that lieutenant where to get off. I'd follow Chase wherever he leads, but MacArthur is just a glory hound, not a leader." There were 'yeah' and 'you got that right' noises from up and down the trenches. The General was not well liked by the troops.

By noon the men were hand carrying supplies again. The grade up the mountain was so steep it was impossible for the trucks to navigate it. All supplies had to be hand carried up and casualties hand carried back down.

"What I wouldn't give for one pack mule," Jones complained.

The objective was to advance into the hills on the west side of Tacloban Valley to establish observation posts and command the entrance to the valley. There was an airbase at Tacloban that had been taken by the 8th Cav late the night before.

The enemy owned the other side of the mountain and, there, the troops met the resistance that they hadn't encountered on the beach. Every movement to top the embankment was immediately answered by a heavy barrage of enemy fire from a big gun that swept the ridge top.

The Japanese ground forces had the invading Allies pinned behind Mt. Badian for three days; neither army had the fire power needed to roust the opposition. The Japanese called in their big Navy support guns to gain the advantage. From their high vantage point, George and the others watched the Japanese Navy steaming into Leyte Gulf from the north just as the sun broke. They came into the Bay in two columns, 15 or more battleships, destroyers, and gun boats.

"Look south," somebody hollered. A single file column of heavy battleships and destroyers approached from that direction. "Ours," was pronouncement by a man with field glasses. "It's the U.S. Navy, by God."

The U.S. task force came up between the two Japanese columns and began firing. The Japanese could not return fire because if they missed their target they were in danger of hitting their own ships. The boom of the guns went on all day. "They're like sitting ducks" the soldiers kept telling each other as they watched the American's sink one after another of the Japanese fleet.

When the smoke cleared, the U.S. Navy had sunk two thirds of the Japanese fleet, but the Japanese ground troops continued to pin the Allies on the far side of Mt. Badian with the sweep of their big gun hidden somewhere on the other side of the valley.

On the day after the naval battle a large man, his face sunburned, his hair bleached white blonde approached George.

"Are you Pvt. Lewis?"

"Yes, Sir," George replied.

"I want to know exactly where that gun is,"

"Stick your head up higher," George said. "They'll shoot at it."

"No, I'm serious," the man replied. "I'm Jake Peevy and I've been sent here to take that gun out. I need to pinpoint the exact location before we call the bombers in. They tell me you'll be able to spot the place they have it hidden."

Peevy was accompanied by a staff sergeant who carried the radio. "This here's Sam," Peevy introduced him.

George crawled cautiously forward, leading the lieutenant and Sgt. Sam to the very top of the ridge. Sure enough, their movement drew enemy fire but the shell fell short, exploding a rock ledge below them.

"Did you see where it came from?" George asked. The lieutenant shook his head. George had spotted the well camouflaged bunker immediately. Its colors may have blended into the jungle greens and browns perfectly, but for a man who was color blind it was visible because of the different way the material reflected light.

"There," George said, "to our right, and left of the peak."

"Bring up those aiming sticks, Sam," Peevy called. Sam handed him two white sticks, which Peevy handed to George. "You line these up with the target."

The big gun fired again and the trio dropped flat on the ground. The shell hit the hillside and exploded six feet in front of them. Peevy was up immediately.

"Double check me, private. Are those stakes lined up on the target?"

George got behind the stakes, sighted down at the camouflaged entrance to the cave and corrected a little. Peevy wore a sensor for the B25 pilots to hone in on. Sgt. Sam cranked up the radio and Peevy called into the mike "Ready." They laid back down and waited. In less than ten minutes they heard a rumble behind them. Three B25 bombers came in single file over the hill. Peevy stood up and stationed himself directly behind the aiming stakes.

George rolled over on his back to watch. Holy socks they were close. He could have scratched a match on their bellies if he'd reached up. Their bomb bays were open and he looked right inside. The lead plane nosed down as it cleared their position and the lieutenant, keeping his eyes on the stakes, yelled "Now."

The bombardier released a bomb that exploded on impact. "High Right," Peevy shouted into the radio. The bomb from the second plane went directly into the cave where the big gun was.

Peevy radioed to the third plane, "Take it home, we don't need it."

"I can't land with a live egg," the pilot called back. "This one is for good measure." The third bomb hit the cave and an ammunition dump exploded. The whole face of the mountain quivered for 30, maybe 40 seconds, and fell into the ravine.

The troops immediately began to advance over the ridge with only sporadic small arms fire to contend with. George led his squad to examine the remains of the cave. The gun had been an American 16mm shore defensive cannon the Japs had captured somewhere. It was mounted on a railroad track and could be rolled out to fire and then withdrawn back into the cave. Now it looked more like a heap of scrap metal in the middle of a scatter of dead bodies.

LEYTE ISLAND - TWO

George opened his eyes and looked around him. It was nighttime but the darkness was not total. A red blackout light was burning somewhere. Where was he? On a cot. He hadn't slept on a cot since they'd left Australia. There were others in the space with him, he could hear breathing and restless bodies turning. When his eyes adjusted to the dim light he could make out rows of cots in a large tent. He was thirsty. He tried to sit up and was surprised at his weakness. Out of the dimness a woman in uniform came to his side.

"Where am I?" he asked as she bent over him.

"Field hospital," she whispered. "How do you feel?"

"Am I wounded?" George wanted to know. His feet burned but nothing else felt different.

"You've been out of your head with malaria for the last three days," she said. "Are you thirsty?"

"And how," George said. The nurse handed him a glass of water.

"Sip slowly," she instructed. "Too much too soon will just make you vomit. Let me look at those feet."

She flipped the light sheet back and lifted first one foot and then the other. "Jungle rot," she explained, shaking her head slowly. "One of the worse cases I've seen. Why didn't you report to a medic with this? If it hadn't been for your malaria attack you would've kept on with it wouldn't you?"

George didn't respond. He was starting to shiver. "I'm cold," he said. Even the words shivered as he said them.

Adding blankets would not heat the malaria victim, but the nurse added a blanket just for the psychological effect it had on the patient. Malaria alternates between high fever and chills. George had been in and out of both since having been admitted to the field hospital. The attack could end as suddenly as it came on, but was apt to recur without notice. Some victims died, some never had another recurrence. He heard a voice to his left.

"Jiggs," it called softly. "Do you remember the night we hopped a freight train for the first time?" It was Farley. George tried to concentrate on the voice as it went on, but he heard only parts of it was he hugged his arms around himself and tried to still the shivering. There were three nurses around him now, trying to warm his body with warm moist towels.

Slowly the heat returned to his limbs and he relaxed. Farley was still talking about the hobo jungle in Milwaukee where they'd spent a couple of months in the spring of 1934. It was daylight now. He turned his head to look at Farley.

"Hi," he said, his voice weak from the ordeal. "Do you have this thing too?"

"Just the jungle rot," Farley said. "A lot of us have it. Probably from wading the swamps the first day."

"We still on Leyte?"

"Yeah, but just some mopping up operations still going on. You didn't miss anything."

Two days later was Christmas day. George had not suffered any more malaria attacks but the infection that had been eating at his toes was not much better. Walking barefoot on the wooden floors of the hospital tent was bearable, but putting on combat boots was not. George and Farley played cribbage while they digested the Christmas dinner of turkey and dressing with sweet potatoes. Nurse Jane, the slightly plump day nurse, asked George if he felt up to having a visitor.

"Of course," said George. "As long as it isn't my first sergeant."

"Says he's your cousin," Jane said.

A minute later a man in Navy uniform came in.

"Eddie," George raised his hand so his cousin could locate him. "Over here."

"Heard you were with the 1st Cav," Eddie said, "So I asked around about you. Sorry to hear you been sick."

George dismissed his concern. "Fine now, except for the jungle rot. They don't seem to have any cure for it."

"I've got something abroad ship that might help," Eddie said. "I'll have it sent to you." They talked for almost an hour, catching up on family news and swapping battle stories. Eddie had been on one of the battleships that took part in the Leyte Gulf victory. He told them about the battle from his perspective and they told him what the 1st Cav had seen from the top of Mt. Badian.

The next morning, Nurse Jane brought a package to George. "A sailor said this was for you," she told him.

George opened the small package. Inside were two bottles of Mennen's After-shave and a note. "Rub this stuff on your burning feet three times a day. It'll hurt like hell, but you'll smell good for the nurses and it'll heal you up quick."

The next evening, just before dusk, a man was shot by a sniper as he walked across the hospital compound. The harassing gunfire went on until dark. At dawn, it started again.

"There are at least three of them," George said. Farley agreed. They were using the Japanese 25-caliber machine gun the men called a woodpecker. They shot fast and accurate and sounded just like a woodpecker at work. The sniper fire became predictable, occurring an hour before dusk and hour after dawn. "Why don't they send a patrol out to get those guys?" Farley wondered.

Three days after Eddie's gift of Mennen's After-shave, a doctor appeared at their bedside along with the nurse. "Let's have a look at that jungle rot," he said to George.

"I think it's about cleared up," George said, sticking his foot out for the doctor to examine.

"I'd agree," the doctor said. "What I want to know is why."

"We been slapping this stuff on," George said, holding out the nearly empty second bottle of the after-shave.

"Where'd you get this?"

George told him about Eddie coming ashore from one of the battleships on R and R. "Mind if I take this for a while?" the doctor asked. "I want to get our supply clerk to get several cases of this stuff. It might solve our biggest problem here."

"Can we get outta here?" Farley asked.

"One or two more days," the doctor said. "You can put on some shoes and socks and try walking around today. White socks only. You'll need a note from me to your sergeant so he doesn't get on you about being out of uniform. We'll examine those feet again tomorrow."

The field hospital was located at the entrance to a horseshoe shaped valley. High hills sloped up from a valley floor that was from 25 to 75 yards wide. A two-track dirt road along the valley floor gave access to a native village at the far end. The valley was less than two miles long. This had to be where the snipers were hiding.

A patrol was organized to locate the snipers. About 60 men, office workers, corpsmen, drivers, and supply clerks were assembled. The patrol was to be led by a young Lt. Basker who had no combat experience. He appeared at the door to the hospital tent and asked for Pvt. Lewis and Pvt. Farley.

"Here, Sir," Farley called.

The lieutenant introduced himself. "I'm sure you've heard our Jap snipers," he said. "I've organized a patrol, but I don't have anybody with combat or jungle experience. Doc Watson said you two might be willing to help out. I can't order you, of course, because you're still patients, but you could volunteer."

George looked at the young lieutenant. It was plain to see the man was scared. "OK," George said, "I'll help."

"I'm in," Farley said.

The men assembled for the patrol were definitely not combat ready. "Divide the patrol in half," George advised Basker. "Let Farley review patrol procedures with half of them and I'll take the rest."

Basker complied and after holding a brief practice patrol session, they moved out. George led his half up the hill on the right, Farley and Basker took a group up the left. They worked their way through the jungle growth along the ridge tops and met three hours later at the far end. Neither group had seen any sign of the snipers. George had scanned the left hillside as he walked the right, looking for camouflaged bunkers. His plan was to walk back on the left rim and scan the right. He was sure he would spot a bunker somewhere.

After a fifteen minute rest, Lt. Basker called "Fall In" ordering the men to assemble in a two-man front formation.

"Are you taking us back in formation on the valley floor?" George asked. "That's crazy, we haven't finished scouting the hills."

"We covered both sides," Basker said. "There's nobody here. We probably scared them out just by showing up."

"Well I won't be a part of a formation down there. Not for you or anybody else. It's too dangerous."

"I order you to get into formation, private," Basker yelled. "I'll have you court-martialed for disobeying orders."

"Fine," George replied. "I'll take my chances with a court-martial."

Farley entered the fray. "I'm with Lewis. Put me on your court-martial list too."

"Insubordination," Basker yelled. "I'll have you hung from a coconut tree."

Basker turned his back on George and Farley and addressed his troops.

"Fall in, right shoulder arms, forward march." and he proceeded to lead the patrol down the hill.

"Which way?" Farley asked George.

"We'll go back the way you came," George said. "I want to see if there are any camouflaged bunkers on the opposite ridge."

From the ridge top, the mutineers watched as the patrol walked the valley floor. Used to walking in the jungle, George and Farley kept just about even with the patrol. Just a little more than half way home, George stopped suddenly, putting a hand on Farley's arm.

"My god," he said pointing across to the other ridge. "There it is." The camouflaged Jap bunker was as evident to George as if it were under a spotlight. "We've got to warn them."

Even as they turned, the woodpeckers opened up. Before George could take three steps, the patrol below them was leveled.

"What'll we do now?" Farley wanted to know.

"We stay hidden and get back to camp," George said. "I can find that bunker again with some decent gunners along."

They reached the field hospital and immediately reported to the CO. Col. Franklin turned to his aide. "Get this typed up and dispatched to headquarters immediately."

Within three hours Gen. William Chase, the division commander, was standing at the foot of Pvt. George Lewis's bed. Col. Franklin, a first sergeant, and a nurse accompanied them.

"I have a report that you encountered difficulty on a patrol," Chase said. "What is your story?"

George started at the beginning when Lt. Basker asked them to volunteer to accompany the patrol. He told Chase about his ability to see through camouflage and how he was looking for the bunker as he went up the valley.

"Did the Lt. know you had this ability?" the General asked.

"Probably not," George said. "I don't generally tell people."

George didn't leave out anything, including the threat of court-martial Lt. Basker had made. He made it clear that he had disobeyed a direct order and had instead walked back along the ridge top.

"When George spotted the bunker, we started to go down to warn them," Farley put it. "But there wasn't time."

The general turned to the first sergeant. "I want an experienced rifle platoon to go in there now."

He turned back to George and Farley. "Would you mind going back with the platoon and pointing out the bunker?"

George sat up. "No, Sir, I don't mind. I can find it, but I doubt if there are any Japs left in it now."

"Are these men able to walk anymore today?" Chase asked Col. Franklin, who was also a doctor.

"Let's take a look," Franklin said. George and Farley presented their feet for inspection. "They look good. If they want to go, I won't stop them."

LEYTE ISLAND -THREE

The next morning, George and Farley were released from the field hospital. The release was accompanied with an order from division headquarters to report to Gen. Chase.

Col. Franklin made a jeep available to them, and they set off for division headquarters. Gen. Chase received them right away. Chase was a tall man, with a distinguished look about him that was serious, but friendly. George and Farley stood before him and saluted.

"At ease," he told them. "I'm told there were no survivors."

"No, sir," George said. "It was the worst thing I've ever seen. They were still in formation, their rifles still slung on their shoulders. The lieutenant was in the lead, of course, and he was probably hit first."

"And from what you told me yesterday, all unnecessary," Gen. Chase said. George was sure he saw the general's eye brighten with tears.

Chase paused for a moment, drew a long breath, and continued. "First, I want you to know no charges are or will be filed against you. If only my junior officers would put their rank aside and listen to a lower ranking person with experience this would not have happened. The patrol should never have been formed of inexperienced people to begin with. They could have asked for a rifle platoon to find their snipers."

"Would they have gotten one?" George asked, aware of his impertinence, but unwilling to keep his mouth shut when something needed to be said.

"Eventually," Chase replied. "Point taken."

He made a steeple out of his fingers and leaned forward to speak. "Gentlemen, I have put you both in for a direct field commission. You will go to officer's training school in Australia and be back here as second lieutenants in about 12 weeks."

"Thank you for the offer, General," George said. "But I refuse. Regulations say I must volunteer to be commissioned, and I will not volunteer."

"I'm with Jiggs, Sir," Farley said.

"Jiggs?" asked the general in a surprised voice.

"I'm sorry," Farley said, "I meant Pvt. Lewis, Sir. Jiggs is his nickname."

"And you know regulations?" Chase continued.

"Yes, Sir," George replied. "I've found them useful from time to time."

"Well, that's just amazing. I wish my junior officers knew them. You'd make fine officers and I need them very badly, as you know."

"I wouldn't make a good officer," George said. "I could never order men into a situation I knew would get them killed."

"You wouldn't be expected to," the General said. "You're just the kind of man I need."

"No," George said, "There are times when you have to do it, and I couldn't."

"I'm going to ask you to think this over for a while," Chase said. "I'll send my orderly to get you for lunch with me tomorrow and we'll discuss it further."

As promised, the general's jeep pulled into the hospital camp to pick them up for lunch the next day. Although they had been discharged from the hospital, the general had ordered them to stay there until he released them.

The general's driver pulled the jeep up in front of the large tent that served as the Officer's Club. When they were ushered into the Gen. Chase's presence, both men stood at attention and saluted.

"At ease, men," the General said. "Let's dispense with all formalities and just enjoy lunch."

They were joined at lunch by several other officers. The food was exceptional and plentiful. They chatted during lunch. Gen. Chase had graduated from the University of Michigan at Ann Arbor and was pleased to find that George was from Michigan. He wanted to hear about the CCC's.

"Can I call you Jiggs?" he asked at one point. "The name just really seems to suit you."

"Of course," George answered. "All my friends call me Jiggs." Eventually as they swapped stories back and forth, the shooting of Sgt. Grasman's horse came out.

Chase laughed heartily. "I was informed about that incident when it happened. It was an accident, wasn't it?"

"Of course," George replied. "But I can't convince Grasman of that."

"Well, Grasman is one of those bull-headed, by-the-book sergeants," he said. "They're good for basic training, but not much good in the field. Out

here you need common sense and respect for the
soldiers. And that's what you've got that would
make you valuable officers. How about it? Have you
decided to accept my offer?"

Farley answered for both of them. "We talked
it, over, General, we really did. But in the end it
comes back to we don't want to. Isn't that right,
Jiggs?"

"It's like I told you right off, Sir," George said.
"I don't think I'm officer material, and I don't think
I could learn to think like one. Just put me back
out there and let's get this war over with."

"Very well," Chase said. "But I can hand out
one promotion you can't refuse. Come back to my
office with me and I'll have the orders written
promoting you both to permanent corporals. If you
ever change your mind about the field commission,
you only have to let me know."

The next day, they were sent back to
Company C. Kelly was glad to have them back, but
Grasman turned every possible shade of red when
he read the copy of their promotion orders. They
were no longer available to him to assign to extra
detail and he could not reduce them in rank
without the general's permission.

Luck was with Grasman that week. A request
came in for a dispatcher in the motor pool, a perfect
job for a corporal you wanted to keep out of your
way. A dispatcher maintains the records of the
military vehicles, processes requests for vehicles,
and makes sure maintenance is done. Grasman
considered it a boring job, and he remembered
Lewis telling him once that he liked to be kept busy.
Well, sitting behind a desk for eight hours a day

would not keep him busy. He'd be bored to smithereens.

What Grasman hadn't taken into consideration was that Farley's regular detail, when they weren't in combat, was in vehicle maintenance. He had inadvertently put the two friends together.

The motor pool was headquartered in a large tent where Cpl. Lewis kept office. His desk was two planks set across two empty oil drums. On a series of makeshift shelves set up behind him were the vehicle record files.

He'd only been the dispatcher for three days and was still getting acquainted with procedures. Farley and three regular drivers were sitting around the large office area drinking coffee. One of the pluses of this job was the constant supply of good java. One of George's main duties, in fact, was to keep the coffee hot and plentiful.

"Grasman blew it again, didn't he?" Farley said. "I don't think he knows he gave you a perfect assignment."

"And don't tell him," George replied from his position behind the desk, on his knees, looking for the file on Jeep #34448.

A lieutenant in a spotless uniform walked in the door. Farley and the three drivers immediately came to attention and saluted as required, but no one called attention, so George, with his back to the door, continued to search for the necessary file.

The lieutenant hesitated for a moment and then shouted. "Soldier, you are to stand and salute when your lord and master comes into your presence."

George stood and turned quickly. He saw the fresh second lieutenant standing there expecting a salute. George sat down on his chair and just looked at him.

"Soldier, give me your name, rank, and serial number. I'm filing charges against you."

George gave the required information but remained seated. The lieutenant took the names of the other men. "Don't any of you leave," he said and stormed out of the tent.

He was back within three minutes, a triumphant looking Grasman in his wake.

"What happened here, corporal?" Grasman asked. "Did you refuse to salute this man?"

"I would have saluted a lieutenant," George replied, "But he insisted I salute my lord and master. Since I didn't see him, I didn't salute."

"Is that what you said?" Grasman turned and looked up at the taller man in disbelief.

"So what if I did. He's required to come to attention and salute when a superior officer comes into the room. Now, file the charges."

Grasman shook his head. "Ok, Sir, but I certainly don't advise it. Especially not against this man."

A summary court to hear the charges was held within the hour. Maj. Blackmer, who had been at the luncheon Gen. Chase had given for George and Farley, was called to be summary court officer.

The charges were read. Farley had to testify that Cpl. Lewis refused to salute Lt. Fordham. Sgt. Grasman presented the defense, repeating the phrase "lord and master," which had been used in the order.

"Did you use those very words, lieutenant?" the Major said.

"I may have, Sir."

"Then these charges are dismissed. As for you, don't even unpack your bags. Report to division commander, Gen. William Chase before 0230."

George had just returned to the motor pool when a very sheepish Lt. Fordham came in the door. George stood and saluted. "What can I help you with, Sir?" he asked.

"I need a jeep to get to division headquarters."

George took out the paperwork necessary, got the Lieutenant's signature and then called Farley forward.

"Take this officer to Gen. Chase. Wait for him and take him wherever the general requests."

Farley had a grin on his face that he couldn't stifle. "Sure thing, Jiggs," he said. "Glad to."

Farley came back that evening with a great tale to tell.

"I listened at Chase's door," he said. "I've never heard anybody so angry. He told Fordham there was no place in his command for arrogant officers and he could take his belonging and orders and get back on the ship he'd come in on. The louie asked where he should go, and the general said he didn't give a shit, just get the hell out of his sight."

Laughter filled the tent. "What'd he do then?" George asked.

"He came back out and got in the jeep, told me to take him down to the harbor. He blew his nose quite often, so I guessed he was fighting tears. Then he said I seemed to be a friend of Cpl. Lewis, wouldn't I intervene on his behalf? He'd apologize, anything, if Cpl. Lewis could talk to Gen. Chase for him so he could stay."

"What'd you say?"

"Well, I told him you had no influence with the general. And he said he'd heard that wasn't true. Grasman told him how you turned down the direct field commission he'd offered, so he thought you could persuade Chase to let him stay."

"I wouldn't have done it," George said. "He was just like Lt. Basker, green behind the gills and arrogant as hell. I say, good riddance."

MANILA, THE PHILIPPINES
February 1945 - September 1945

MANILA - ONE

On 1 February 1945, the 1st Cavalry Division landed on the Philippine capital island of Luzon. The island had already been invaded by allied troops in early January, so the landing of the Cavalry was unopposed.

Many American, British, and Allied nationals were in concentration camps in Manila. Gen. MacArthur had assigned Gen. Chase and his 1st Cavalry to take Manila as quickly as possible and free those prisoners. Intelligence reports indicated that the prisoners would likely be killed as the Allied Armies approached Manila. Chase took the 5th Cavalry and began his "Dash for Manila". The 12th Cav followed closely on his heels.

The approach to Manila was heavily opposed by the Japanese. They were setting fire to many of the buildings behind them as they retreated into the heart of the city. Company C advanced slowly, taking the city practically one house at time.

George and his troop had spent the night in shallow fox holes hidden behind some shrubbery in the front yard of a small white house. Their machine gun sat on its tripod ready to provide cover for the advancing riflemen when needed.

Just before dawn, the door of the house opened and a smiling Filipino came out with a pot of steaming coffee. "May I serve you coffee?" he asked.

"Coffee?" Farley answered, a hopeful lilt in his voice.

"Thank you," George said, "but food must be hard to get here. Surely you should keep such a precious thing for yourself."

"No problem," the man said. "When the Japs came, we neighbors all buried coffee and other good stuff in this yard. Your gun sits on top of our remaining coffee stash, but we have enough now to give you and all the men a morning drink."

As they drank their coffee, the Filipino wanted to talk. "We knew you were coming," he said. "Two days ago the Japs made the whole town go to Rizal Stadium for a meeting. The big man talking told us we had better stick with them because Luzon was now part of the Land of the Rising Sun empire."

The man paused and a big grin split his face. "This part is funny," he said. "Just like a picture show. The man talking said to us, 'you'll never see another American plane in these skies.' He waved his hand while he said this and pointed directly at a formation of American P38's. They pretty much broke up the Jap's meeting as everybody ran for cover." The man laughed aloud and said, "So glad you are here. Coffee for Americans anytime, even if it was my last cup."

Thus fortified, the Platoon moved forward as soon as dawn broke. They moved cautiously for about two blocks, before gunfire from a large two story fire station ahead stopped their advance. It took almost two hours for the Cavalry men to enter the building.

Inside the station was a long LaFrance ladder truck. Farley jumped into the cab and started it up. It was already headed out. "Jump on the rear and steer for me, Jiggs," he shouted.

Without giving it a second thought, George leaped onto to moving truck. Farley held his foot to the gas pedal while George clung to the back, trying to make the rear end follow the front end as they raced down the winding streets back out of the city. As they progressed, several jeeps carrying MP's began to chase them. It all came to a screeching halt when they reached a roadblock in front of division headquarters.

The first man out of the jeeps to confront the fire truck was a Bird Colonel.

"Where do you think you're going?" he demanded.

"We just captured this up front," Farley said. "We thought it would be useful so we brought it back here for safe keeping."

The colonel nodded. "Very commendable, if a little unusual. What outfit you men with?"

George had come forward and said, "Company C, 12th Cavalry, Sir. We've been fighting house to house for a couple days now and the fire-truck was a trophy too good to pass up."

"Can somebody take us back to our outfit," Farley asked, pressing his luck.

"Sure thing, corporal," the colonel replied. "Jump in."

They approached the fire-station with the colonel. Grasman had watched them leave and shouted for the MP's to give chase. Now he was waiting eagerly to confront the general's pets. He had them dead to rights this time. Before the jeep even came to a halt he was running alongside screaming court-martial, desertion, firing-squad, and anything else he could think of including the usual insubordinate bastard directed at George.

Capt. Kelly had observed that the returning men were accompanied by a bird colonel and ran forward to put himself between the colonel and Sgt. Grasman.

"Capt. Kelly," the colonel said as they exchanged salutes. He introduced himself. "You've got two very good men here and I want to commend them. They've saved a very valuable piece of equipment for us."

He turned to get back in his jeep then stopped in front of a red-faced Sgt. Grasman. He shook a finger in his face and said, "No way," meaning don't even think of filing charges.

George and Farley made themselves scarce as soon as the colonel got in his jeep.

"I think Grasman just did us a favor," George said.

"How so?" inquired Farley.

"If he hadn't been on our backs when we came in, I think the colonel might have recommended at least a mild reprimand for us. As it was, we were commended."

"I sure wish he'd put it in writing," said Farley. "Every point counts you know. I was looking at our point count and we're both almost at the limit. Any luck at all and we'll be on the first boat home."

"I'm not so sure," George said. "Scuttlebutt says everybody goes to Japan next.

MANILA – TWO

The closer the G.I.'s got to the center of Manila, the fiercer the battles for each building. Each room seemed to be occupied by at least one Jap soldier, sometimes two. When a soldier opened the door, the Jap inside would rush forward, shooting as he came. Standard procedure was to open the door and toss in a grenade which the Jap would rush into and be blown to pieces with the door. As the battle progressed, the Japs got smarter and waited against the back wall until the grenade exploded. The American's in turn got smarter, following up the first grenade with a second.

It took nine days to take the last three blocks. Casualties were as high as 50 percent in some units.

George had never been so tired. He could take a nap at a moment's notice, while somebody who had just caught 40 winks kept guard. During one lull while he kept watch so the rest of the squad could nap, he reflected on how things had changed since Liska had died. Then he had been appalled at the reality of seeing dead men. He, and the others, now casually stepped over bodies, sometimes even kicked them aside if they were in the way. They'd lost Jerry Cribar and Nebraska Jim. George didn't know if they were dead or wounded. The smell of death was everywhere. In the tropical heat and humidity, bodies started to decay within hours and maggots appeared almost immediately. George figured the only thing that kept him and his men going was desperation and fatigue.

The Imperial Hotel in the heart of downtown had been used by the Japanese High Command as their headquarters, and as Gen. MacArthur's before them. It was the final stronghold as the Cav pressed forward, and Capt. Kelly's Charlie Company had been designated to take it. After the first floor was cleared out, George and the three men left in his squad were sent to clear out the basement. They used the two grenade concept, proceeding slowly into the east end while another squad worked their way west.

"Only one room left," Farley said. "Then maybe we can take a break."

"Let's take the room first," George said. "Then we'll talk about breaks." He turned to Jones who was following right on his heels. "OK, I'll work the door, you toss. Farley, you be ready with the second one. I'll go in first."

The grenades worked. They entered the room to find two very young Jap soldiers laying on the floor. One of them moved slightly and George pulled the trigger.

He heard the Browning Automatic Rifle (BAR) Jones was carrying open up behind him. Looking ahead he saw there were two more Japs coming at them from a second door that opened into the first room. They fell even as he saw them.

He threw a grenade into the second room and got another Jap coming through yet another door opening off the second room.

"Grenade," George hollered, "there might be more,". Franco was right there with another grenade that he lobbed into the third room, followed by another. Farley entered the room first, George covered him with his BAR ready.

"No more," Farley shouted. "But would you look at this?"

"Holy socks," George said as he looked around him. "This room is full of whiskey." There were cases and cases of it piled nearly to the ceiling. Most of the boxes were labeled Old Granddad

"There's more back there," Jones said, indicating the first and second rooms.

They backtracked. All three rooms were filled with cases of American whiskey. The first room had mostly Four Roses, the second some Dewers Scotch and more Four Roses, and the third, the choice Old Granddad.

From above them they could still hear the bursting of grenades and constant gunfire. Some of the whiskey bottles had been shattered by flying shrapnel and the pungent sweet smell of whiskey filled the room. For the first time in ten days, there was no death smell.

Jigg's first thought was how to keep the men out of the whiskey. "Jones," he said. "You and Franco hightail it to Capt. Kelly and tell him what we got here and find out what he wants us to do about it."

With them gone he turned to Farley. "OK, Farley. It's up to us to guard that door and keep everybody out until the captain gets here."

Sgt. Grasman was the first to show up. "What have we got here, Lewis?"

"Three rooms full of American Whiskey," George answered.

"OK," Grasman said looking around, "You and Farley can leave, I'll take care of this."

"I've sent for Capt. Kelly," George said. "We'll stay until he comes. One man won't be able to keep the men out if they decide they want the booze."

"You're dismissed," Grasman repeated. "That's an order."

For the second time in his career, Grasman heard Capt. Kelly say, "I'm going to rescind that order, sergeant."

The captain was accompanied by three men in addition to Jones and Franco. He walked through all three rooms and shook his head. "I wonder why the Japs didn't have it all drunk up by now?"

"They may have thought it was poisoned," Franco said. "I've heard they were paranoid that way."

"Do you want me to post a guard on the rooms, Captain?" Grasman asked.

"I think Cpls. Lewis and Farley can handle this." Capt. Kelly said. "You are dismissed, sergeant.

Turning to the rifle squad he said, "I'm leaving you on 24-hour guard. Nobody is to touch the whiskey until I return. You may shoot anyone who attempts to."

"Yes, Sir," George said, giving a rifle salute. "We'll take care of it."

The men had been fighting for almost ten days with very little sleep. George and Farley decided on alternating four-hour watches. George and Franco took the first watch while Farley and Jones got some real sleep behind the closed door of the second room.

The two men on watch had no trouble staying awake. Every ten minutes or so, somebody came to the door and wanted to take 'just one bottle'. On one occasion two lieutenants showed up and tried to pull rank.

"Captain's orders," George said racking a shell into the magazine of his rifle. They left.

Finally George and Franco got their chance to sleep. It took about two seconds for them to fall asleep while Farley and Jones stood guard at the whiskey room door.

Just as George and Franco were starting their second shift on guard, Grasman showed up again. DeeDee Whitmore and another man were with him.

"You guys want to take a break? We'll take a turn," Grasman said.

"We're doing all right," George said. "Besides, the captain gave express orders to me and Farley to maintain a 24-hour guard." Grasman turned to leave and George called after him. "Some coffee would be welcome if you can find some."

An hour later, Grasman and Whitmore were back. Grasman had a cup of coffee, which he offered to George and then pulled it back. "Cup of coffee for one bottle," he said.

"No way," George answered.

"Look, Lewis," Grasman said. "I'm First Sergeant here and nobody's gonna miss one or two bottles." He set the coffee on the stack of cases.

"Just let me look at it." He ripped open a case and lifted two bottles out. He handed them to Whitmore and took out two more. Then he made a move for the door.

"Put it back," George warned. He racked a shell into the magazine.

"You wouldn't dare," Grasman said. "You'll shoot a poor defenseless horse, but you won't shoot me."

"Try me," George said, shoving the muzzle of the rifle into Grasman's stomach.

Whitmore made a dash for the door. Franco used the stock of his .030 to hit him on the back of the head. DeeDee slumped to the floor. One of the bottles of Four Roses he held broke on impact. "Farley," George yelled. "Get out here."

Farley and Jones burst into the room with rifles ready. Farley took in the situation immediately.

"Go get the captain," Farley said to Jones. "Tell him we've had to shoot a couple of men for disobeying his orders."

Grasman held the two bottles out to Farley. "Here, take them," he said. "I wasn't gonna take 'em. I was only looking."

"Keep your hands right there," George said. "And don't drop those bottles. It smells bad enough in here already."

They waited in silence until Farley asked. "You notice anything?"

"What?"

"The shooting's stopped, the building must be secured."

"Somebody's coming down the hallway," George said, "Cover the door, Franco."

"It's the captain," Franco called over his shoulder. "Looks like he has some brass with him."

Farley and Franco saluted as Capt. Kelly, Col. Edwards, and Gen. Chase entered the room. George kept his rifle on Grasman's stomach.

After a guard had taken Grasman and Whitmore away, Gen. Chase addressed George.

"So, we meet again Jiggs. And you once again fulfill my expectations for an exemplary junior officer."

"Just doing my job, Sir," George replied.

The officers walked through the three rooms. When they returned, Chase addressed George again.

"What do you think we should do with it, Jiggs?"

"Well," George rubbed his chin as he formulated his answer. He hadn't shaved in two weeks and the beard on his chin was substantial. "Word's around that the whiskey is here. We've had a steady stream of visitors. The expected thing is that you'll take it for the officers."

He stopped talking and looked around the room. "Sure wish it was beer," he said. "I'm not a whiskey drinker myself." Another pause and then he continued.

"It sounds like we've cleared the Japs outta town. I don't hear much gunfire. I think you should give a bottle to each squad. That's not enough to get them drunk, but it's enough to let them know you appreciate the job we did here."

"Excellent idea," Chase exclaimed. "What do you think, Jack?" he asked Col. Edwards.

"I agree," the Colonel replied. "And I have a case a beer for this man who doesn't like whiskey."

MANILLA – THREE

Harry Grasman couldn't believe this was happening to him. It was bad enough to be pinned against the wall by that bastard, Lewis, but when Gen. Chase and Col. Edward walked in with Capt. Kelly his heart sank. If it had been just Kelly he had been prepared to talk his way out of this mess.

Kelly wasted no time. "Sgt. Grasman you are under arrest for disobeying orders." And then Lewis, the bastard, had reached over and taken his .45 from its holster and then the two bottles of whiskey he still held.

"I'll need those as evidence," Kelly said to George. George handed them over Capt. Kelly. Then Kelly turned to two of men who had come in with him. "Sergeant, take these two men to the MP's."

Grasman and Whitmore had to walk up the stairs and out of the building ahead of the armed guards. It seemed as through the entire Company was standing around watching them. Whitmore kept his head down, but Grasman had looked his men right in the eye as he passed.

There was a troop carrier waiting outside with driver. The guards ushered Grasman and Whitmore into the back-end and got in behind them. They were driven to command headquarters and put in a tent with guards posted front and rear.

As soon as they were alone, Whitmore began to rant and rave about Lewis. "Oh, just shut up," Grasman said. "I don't even want to hear that bastard's name."

Two hours later, a man approached the front door guard. They conferred a moment and then the guard came inside. "Corporal," he said. "There are no charges against you. You may leave."

"What about me?" Grasman asked.

"No word about you," the guard said and exited the tent leaving Grasman alone. It was hot inside. The temperature was at least 110 and humid.

"How about some water?" he called. The guard passed him a canteen of water without a word. "Do I get lunch?"

"Later," the guard said. "It's only 1100 hours."

Late in the afternoon, a captain entered the tent. "Sgt. Grasman, I'm Capt. Hillier and I've been appointed your defense advocate."

"I don't have much of a defense, do I?" Grasman asked.

"You tell me," Hillier said. He straddled the second chair, leaned his chin on his folded hands and said. "What happened?"

Grasman stared at the captain in front of him for a long time. "Would it do any good to prove that Lewis is an insubordinate bastard?"

"Whoever Lewis is, he isn't on trial. You are."

Then Grasman said, "I went downstairs and offered to relieve Lewis and his men. They'd been on guard duty for almost twelve hours. Lewis asked me to get him some coffee. He implied that if I got him some coffee, I could have one bottle of whiskey. But when I came back with the coffee, he threatened to shoot me when I picked up the whiskey."

"Do you have a witness who can swear Lewis promised you a bottle in exchange for the coffee?"

"Corporal Duane Whitmore." Grasman answered.

"That the man who was with you?"

"Yes."

"It won't work, Grasman. I've already talked to him and his story says nothing about Lewis promising you a bottle for a cup of coffee. In fact, what he said," Hillier opened a small notebook, "yes, here it is. He said that you went to get Lewis some coffee in hopes that you could trade it for a bottle."

Grasman ran a finger down his scar. "Yeah," he admitted. "That's the way it was."

Court convened at 0900 on the second day after charges were filed. The hearing was held in the officers mess tent at division headquarters. A panel of three officers had been selected to hear the charges: two majors and a lieutenant colonel. In addition an advisory panel of six enlisted men was appointed to hear the case. By the time the MP's escorted Grasman into the room, the Judges and the peer panel had already introduced themselves.

There were four sergeants and two corporals on the advisory panel. None of them were from Company C, but Grasman recognized all four of the sergeants. In the brief time he had to look around the room he saw Lewis and his squad, Capt. Kelly, Gen. Chase, Col. Edwards, and Duane Whitmore all sitting on the prosecution side of the room.

Lt. Col. Fred Evans asked the defendant to stand. "State your name, rank, serial number, and company," he said.

"Harold Grasman, First Sergeant, 234-11-4452, 12the Cavalry, Company C, Sir." He felt Hillier's hand urging him to sit down again.

"Is the defendant represented by an advocate?"

Capt. Hillier stood. "Yes, Sir."

"State your name, rank, serial number and qualifications" one of the Majors said.

"Jeff Hillier, Captain, 432-33-7799. I graduated from University of Missouri law school in 1938."

The Judge's Advocate, Maj. Betts, was called to identify himself next.

Maj. Slater, to the right of the Col. asked Grasman to stand. Hillier stood next to him. "Sgt. Grasman, you are charged with disobeying a direct order of a commission officer and possession of illegal contraband. Do you understand these charges?"

"Yes, sir", Grasman said quietly.

"How do you plead?"

"He pleads guilty, Sir," Hillier said.

"Is that correct?" the major asked Grasman directly.

"Yes, Sir," Grasman replied.

"Tell the court in your own words what the order was and what you did."

Grasman hung his head for a moment and then began to speak. "When Cpl. Lewis and his men found the rooms full of whiskey at the Imperial Hotel, Capt. Kelly, Commanding Officer of Company C, put Cpl. Lewis and his squad in charge of guarding the whiskey until he returned. Lewis was told he had authority to shoot anyone who took any." He stopped talking, suddenly confused about what he should say next.

"Did you actually hear Capt. Kelly give this command?" one of the Majors prompted.

"Yes."

"And did you subsequently attempt to remove whiskey from the room,"

"I did," Grasman admitted.

"Did the guard challenge you?"

"Yes."

"Did you offer to put the whiskey back?"

"No."

"Thank you, sergeant, you may sit down."

The three judges conferred together briefly and then Lt. Col. Evans spoke.

"The defendant has pleaded guilty so no further proceedings are necessary." He turned to the defense table.

"Will the defendant please stand. Harry Grasman, I have no choice but to reduce you to the rank of corporal. Because this was a non-violent crime, there will be no guard- house time. We are recommending you for transfer back to the states. You will receive orders to report to the next ship going to San Francisco. Until that time you are attached to headquarters company."

MANILLA - FOUR

"I don't like warm beer," Farley complained, prying the cap off his third bottle.

"The English prefer it this way," George said, holding his amber colored bottle up to the light and squinting through it. "My sister wrote me that," he added when he noticed Jones looking at him with a skeptical eye.

"I thought maybe you read it somewhere and committed it to memory," Jones answered.

"Deal the cards," Farley ordered. "We've only got 'til midnight."

It was 110 degrees. The city stank of death and buzzed with insect noise. Flies were everywhere. Every bit of shade was cluttered with bunches of three to ten soldiers, each with their whiskey allotment. True to his word, Col. Edward had a sent half a case of Pasbt Blue Ribbon beer to George. His squad was sitting in the shade of the hotel drinking and playing four-handed cribbage.

"Leave me out," George said. "This warm beer in making me nauseous and my head aches."

"You can't quit in the middle," Jones said, but when he looked at George he knew he wasn't faking.

"We'll play three handed," Farley said. "You take a nap, Jiggs."

George lay down on his back and stared up at the white exterior of the hotel. It shimmered in the heat and he could hear his heart pounding in his ears. It felt like his brains were trying to bust out of his eyeballs. He pressed his hands against his temples, trying to press the pain away. A wave of nausea swept over him and he bolted upright, sure the beer was about to be upchucked. The sudden movement heightened the pain in his head which now seemed to ricochet from wall to wall.

"You OK, Jiggs?" Farley said, close by. George couldn't' tell where.

"Sure," he managed and slowly lay back down. He finally slept. Some time later he awoke with a jerk. My god, it had turned cold. It was dark and he heard only muffled sounds around him.

"Farley," he called. His voice seemed no more than a whisper. He tried again, shivering with a sudden violent chill. "Farley!"

"Here," a voice from far away responded. "My god, Jiggs what's the matter?"

"Cold," George reported through shaking lips.

George was moved to a field hospital. The malaria attack alternated between chills and fever for three days. On the third day, the fever was intense but there was no sweating; instead George's breathing was rapid and came in pants. Finally the sweat began to flow out of every pore and then his temperature dropped to normal. Like the first attack, it left him exhausted.

The next morning, after a sponge bath, the ward nurse came up to his bed.

"Do you want a visitor?" she asked him.

George nodded. He heard the nurse say. "Don't stay long, he's awfully tired."

It was Gen. Chase. "Well, Jiggs," he said. "You've had a rough time of it and I'm told this isn't the first time malaria has laid you low."

"No Sir," George replied, making a feeble attempt to salute.

"I've filled out papers for your medical discharge," he said. "There's a ship sailing day after tomorrow, has a hospital ward, and you'll be on it. I just stopped by to said good-bye and thank you for being here."

"Thank you, Sir," George said, aware he was smiling. "I'll be glad to get home."

The general George extended his hand waving aside a salute, and then turned to go.

"Wait," George called.

Chase turned.

"How about Rizal?"

"The stadium?" Chase answered. "The tanks came up first and fired point-blank at the stadium wall until they had blasted a hole big enough for the bulldozers to get through.

"When the troops entered, the place was littered with dead Japanese. They had all died of wounds or suicide. The place smelled of rotting flesh."

He paused. "Maybe we should thank you for that, the 24-hour whiskey delay allowed many of the Japanese to escape, and the rest killed themselves. The city is secured."

Farley, Jones and Franco came by to say goodbye.

"We saw Nebraska Jim," Jones said. "He'll be back on duty by next week."

"What about Jerry?" George asked.

"Dead," Farley said. "Haven't been able to find out details."

"I don't want to know," George said. "Of all the death we've seen, I still have nightmares about Liska. Kid like that never should have been over here.'"

"Tomorrow we start training again," Jones said. "We've been chosen to invade Japan. You're lucky you're going home."

George spent the first ten days at sea in the hospital ward. He had a chance to read the contents of the envelope Capt. Kelly had handed him when he came to say goodbye. It was a commendation for "heroic duty in the taking of Manila," signed by both Capt. Kelly and Gen. Chase. He reviewed the last four years in his mind. He recalled the trip over three years before, when Grasman had had them doing galley duty most of time. Too bad about ol' Grasman. Maybe he was peeling spuds now.

One day out of San Francisco, George wandered along the deck and encountered Grasman sitting there, staring out to sea.

"Hello," George said in surprise.

Grasman squinted into the sun trying to see who it was.

When he recognized George, he spat onto the deck. "What the hell are you doing here?" he asked.

"Being sent home on account of my malaria," George said. "Mind if I sit down?"

"You'll do it no matter what I say. You've been an insubordinate bastard from the first." There was a tone of resignation in his voice.

George remained standing and lit a cigarette. He offered one to Grasman, which he refused.

"Look, Sarge," George used his former rank out of habit, "I know you don't believe it, but shooting Dolly was truly an accident. She was a beautiful animal and I still have nightmares about that day."

"She wasn't your horse," Grasman leapt to his feet and shouted, "You killed her."

George shook his head. "I warned you I wasn't familiar with your horse," George answered, keeping his voice calm. "But you wouldn't listen. It's an order you said. You had to have the beer, just like you had to have the whiskey."

"You bastard," Grasman said, shaking his fist in George's face. "You god-damned insubordinate bastard." He turned and ran along the deck, stumbled once and grabbed the rail for balance. He stood a moment and then ran on.

George watched him go. He was almost home, but so much had been lost in the last four years. So much.

THE END

About the Author

While still Controller and VP of Finance for a steel service center in Grand Rapids, Michigan, Janet Flickinger-Bonarski was, at heart, a writer. When she attended a Writers Workshop at the University of Iowa, she couldn't understand

why people were puzzled that she could be a precise accountant **and** a creative writer. There may be a slight betrayal of her left-brained sense of order in her tight, no excess words writing style, but there is a lot of right-brained creativity evident in the stories she tells.

Now that she is retired, the creative side is evident not only in the novels and short stories she writes, but in the beautiful quilts she makes. "Quilting defined my mother, and she passed that passion on to her four daughters, all of whom have made at least one full size quilt.

When Janet and her husband, Richard, moved to Gaylord after retirement, Janet says she felt like she had come home. Well, half-way home. Her mother was born and raised in Wolverine and her great-grandfather, Frank Randolph, was a pioneer of Vanderbilt, but the Garden Peninsula in Upper Michigan is where Janet was raised. "This is as far north as I could get my husband," she says. "It's halfway between three of our sons in Grand Rapids, and my three sisters in Upper Michigan."

Janet is already a quarter of the way through her next novel which has the working title "**Against the Wind**." It's set in the 1880's in the old Iron smelting town of Fayette. Fayette, now a ghost town on beautiful Snail Shell Harbor on the Garden Peninsula, is a Michigan State park. The same Gerald Willet who was the model for her hero in "**Insubordinate Bastard**." worked on the early restoration of the ghost town.

Janet has four sons and five grandchildren. Her husband of 40 years "is very supportive of everything I do," she says.

Frank Willet, younger brother of Gerald Willet, collaborated with the author in the writing of this book. He contributed his expertise on military procedures, his own experience in the South Pacific during WWII, and a more detailed knowledge of the stories Gerald had shared with him. After serving in WWII as a radio-communications tech in the Army, he re-enlisted in the Air Force and made it his career. He was on recruiting duty in Marquette, Michigan during their Centennial celebration and had to get special permission from Col. Hubbard, commander of Michigan recruiting services, who had to get permission from the two-star general in Chicago who was commander of the sixth army, to grow the beard. He did not win the contest.

Frank is now retired and lives in Shell Knob, Missouri.

Sergeant Frank N. Willet
Marquette, Michigan Centennial celebration
1949

45th Parallel Publishing Co.

**Half way between the Equator and the North Pole
Publishing Michigan Authors**

QUICK ORDER FORM

e-mail orders: <u>Sales@45thparallelpub.com</u>
Fax Orders: 989-731-3402
Postal Orders: 45th Parallel Publishing Co.
                1429 West Main PMB 182
                Gaylord, MI 49735

Please send _____ copies of <u>Insubordinate Bastard</u>

Ship to: _____

_____

_____

The author will be happy to autograph any books ordered from the publisher. Include the name you wish the author to use to personalize your copy for yourself or for gifts.

_____ books @ 14.95 each _____

Michigan residents include 6% sales tax _____

Shipping and Handling $3.95 per book _____

                Total Amount Due _____

Payment: Check ____   Credit Card _____

Card Number _____

Name on Card _____ Exp. Date _____

Signature _____

Visit our Web Site at <u>WWW.45thParallelPub.Com</u> for Author Tour information and updates on other books by 45th Parallel Publishing Co.